Catherine Farrar

20 Ledston Avenue

Garforth

Leeds

PURNELL
SUNSHINE BOOKS

Titles in this series:

Fireside Tales
Good Night Stories
Fun Time Tales
Every Day Stories

* * *

Anytime Tales
Fairyland Stories
Happy Adventure Tales
Little Animal Stories
Sleepyland Stories
Toyland Tales

* * *

Bedtime Stories
Fairy Stories
Happy Time Stories
Holiday Stories
Rainy Day Stories
Sleepy Time Tales

EVERY DAY STORIES

EVERY DAY STORIES

PURNELL
London

SBN 361 02075 9
Published in 1972 by Purnell, London

Made and printed in Great Britain by Purnell & Sons Ltd.,
Paulton (Somerset) and London

CONTENTS

Little Mrs. Millikin

MRS. MILLIKIN was a tiny old lady who lived in Nod village. She hadn't any children of her own, so she loved everybody else's.

She loved little Peter who lived at the grocer's. She loved Susie Green who lived at the post-office. She loved the baby next door, and she loved the twins across the road, although they were really very naughty sometimes.

And they all loved little Mrs. Millikin. When they saw her coming they ran to her, shouting, "Millikin! Millikin! Have you got a sweet for us? Millikin, tell us a story!"

Mrs. Millikin spent all her money on sweets and toys for other people's children. She made chocolate biscuits every week to put into a tin that she kept for the children when they came to see her. She remembered all their birthdays and bought them cards and presents.

So they loved her very much, and when the twins made her a pin-cushion for her birthday little Mrs. Millikin was so proud of it that she showed it to quite a hundred people. She kept it in the middle of her

mantelpiece and hardly dared to put a pin or needle in it for fear of spoiling it.

Of course, you can imagine that when Christmas-time came Mrs. Millikin went quite mad. She spent all her money on things like balloons and crackers and toys and sweets, and gave them to all the children she knew. She saved up for weeks before so that she could have a really good spend.

Then what a time she had! She went to the toy-shop and bought dolls, toys, and books. She went to the sweet-shop and bought packets of sweets and boxes of chocolate and tins of biscuits. She went to the book-shop and bought all kinds of gay cards. Really, she had a perfectly lovely time—but she was happiest of all when she gave what she had bought to the children, and heard all their squeals of joy and saw their beaming faces.

"That's my best Christmas present," she always said. "That's my very best Christmas present—seeing the children so happy and excited."

Now one Christmas little Mrs. Millikin planned all her presents as usual. Ships for the twins. A doll for Susie Green—one that opened and shut its eyes. Books for Bobby. A rattle for the baby. Oh, she would have a fine time spending all her money!

Little Mrs. Millikin worked very hard to get her money. She scrubbed Mrs. Jones's floors for her. She washed Mrs. Lacy's curtains. She mended Mr. Timm's socks. And by the time Christmas week came she had a purse full of money to spend. So out she went to spend it at the toy-shop and the sweet-shop.

LITTLE MRS. MILLIKIN

And then a really dreadful thing happened! Little Mrs. Millikin had a hole in her skirt pocket and she didn't know it! She put her purse there, and as she walked along to the village, the purse dropped out. Mrs. Millikin didn't hear it fall, so she didn't know.

When she got to the toy-shop she put her hand into her pocket to get out her purse—and it wasn't there! What a shock for her! The tiny old lady ran back along the road to see if she could find it. But she couldn't find it anywhere.

And no wonder she couldn't—for Jim the tramp had spied it on the ground and had picked it up in joy. He had gone off with it, thinking that he would buy himself a really fine Christmas dinner. So little Mrs. Millikin didn't find her purse at all. She was very unhappy.

"Now I can't buy the children any presents," she thought, with tears in her eyes. "The twins must do without their ships—and oh, I did promise to give them one each! And Susie can't have her doll. This is really dreadful!"

She did not think that she would not have any Christmas dinner herself. She had meant to buy something for her own dinner on Christmas Day—now she would have to have bread and jam. But all she worried about was not being able to buy presents for the children.

She went to bed very unhappy on Christmas Eve. She had a very little bed, because she was a very little person. It was a cold night, so she drew the blanket right over her head to keep warm. She didn't go to sleep for a long time, but at last she shut her eyes and fell fast asleep.

Now, as you know, Santa Claus comes along each Christmas Eve and fills the children's stockings with toys. He doesn't bother about the grown-ups, of course—they can buy all they want for themselves.

Well, this Christmas Eve, quite by mistake, Santa Claus went down the wrong chimney. He thought he was going down Susie Green's chimney, and he wasn't. He was going down little Mrs. Millikin's!

When he got down into her bedroom he stared round. This wasn't Susie Green's room. He must have come down the wrong chimney. What a nuisance!

Then he caught sight of little Mrs. Millikin lying on her little tiny bed. She was a very small person, no bigger than a child, and as she had the blanket pulled right up to her hair, Santa Claus couldn't see that she wasn't a child. He quite thought she was, she was so small!

"Now here's a funny thing!" said Santa to himself, turning over the pages of his notebook, till he came to the names of all the children in Nod Village. "Here's a very—funny—thing! I haven't got this child's name down! How lucky that I happened to come down the chimney! This child would have had no presents from me if I hadn't come along to-night by mistake. And that would have been a great pity."

Santa Claus stared at the bed. He wondered if it was a boy or a girl. He didn't know. He couldn't see the face of the sleeping person. He didn't like to pull down the blanket in case he woke up the sleeper.

"Well, I don't really know what to do," said Santa, scratching his head and frowning. "It may be a boy. It may be a girl. It may even be a baby, though it looks rather too big for that. What had I better do? And where's the stocking for me to fill? There doesn't seem to *be* one. So I simply can't tell what child it is—boy, girl, or baby!"

He looked round the little bedroom. He saw a pair of old Mr. Timms's socks that Mrs. Millikin had just washed and darned, and had put ready to take back to him.

"Good!" he said. "Those will do nicely." He unrolled them and hung them at the foot of the little bed. Then he undid his sack and looked inside.

"If it's a boy it will like ships and boats," he said, and he put a ship and a boat into a stocking. "If it's a girl it will like dolls." He put a beautiful doll into the stocking, so that it peeped out at the top. It could open and shut its eyes and it had golden curls and a blue ribbon.

"If it's a baby it will like a rattle," said Santa, and into the stocking went a blue-and-red rattle. Then old Santa dived into his sack again and brought out some books, and an engine, and a race-game.

"I didn't give this child anything at all last year," he thought. "Poor little thing! I'd better make up for it this year."

So he packed into those two big stockings all sorts of lovely things—sweets, biscuits, oranges, nuts, apples, little animals, balls, and even a toy telephone, which he knew most children really loved.

Then up the chimney he went again, and disappeared into the frosty night. Mrs. Millikin heard the bells of the reindeer in her dreams but they didn't wake her up. She didn't open her eyes till the morning —and then how she stared *and* stared!

At the bottom of her bed hung two large stockings. From one peeped a pretty, golden-haired doll. From the other stared a large wooden soldier.

"I must still be asleep," said Mrs. Millikin. "Or else I've gone back to being a child. Which is it?"

She got out of bed and looked at herself in the glass. No—she was still Mrs. Millikin, with curly grey hair and a wrinkled, smiling face!

But it wasn't a dream either. "*Most* peculiar," thought Mrs. Millikin, looking at the stockings again. "It almost looks as if Santa Claus has been here and filled those stockings for me. What shall I do about it?"

And then, of course, she knew quite well what she was going to do about it!

"I'll give all the toys to the children!" she cried. "How pleased they will be! Here are just the things they want—a ship—a boat—an engine—a doll—a rattle—oh, what marvellous things, to be sure!"

You would have been surprised to see how quickly Mrs. Millikin dressed that morning. She was out of the house in fifteen minutes, carrying all the toys. And what a wonderful time she had giving away all those presents! How the children hugged and kissed her!

"What have you got for your Christmas dinner, Millikin?" asked Susie Green, hugging her doll in joy. "We've got turkey and plum pudding. Ooooooh!"

"Well, I've got bread and jam, and that's all," said Mrs. Millikin. "But I shall be just as happy with that as you will with your turkey and plum pudding —because, you see, I've seen so many smiling faces this morning that they are as good as a feast to me."

"Millikin, you must stay and share my dinner!" said Susie. "Mustn't she, Mummy? Do say yes."

"Of course she must!" said Mummy. And Mrs. Millikin had to. Then she went to tea with Bobby, and shared his Christmas tree, so she had a marvellous Christmas after all.

"Best I've ever had!" she said to herself, as she cuddled down into her small bed that night. "Best I've ever had. And I'm sure I don't know what I've done to deserve it."

But I know quite a lot of things, don't you?

The Packet of Sweets

"I SAY!" said Bill, coming into the cloakroom where the others were hanging up their hats and changing their shoes. "I say! Look what I've found!"

The others crowded round. Bill held out a little blue packet. He opened the top of it, and inside the children saw a lot of little round yellow things.

"Sweets!" said Bill. "Somebody bought them and dropped them. I found them out in the road, so I expect they fell from someone's bicycle basket. Have one?"

"But you ought to try to find out who they belong to before you eat them," said Mollie at once.

"Finding's keeping," said Bill.

"It isn't," said George. "You know it isn't. Suppose you found a diamond brooch. Would you say it was yours just because you found it? You'd have to take it to the police station, you know you would."

"Well, I guess the police would laugh if I took these sweets along," said Bill.

"I don't care. You ought to," said George. "Or at least you should hand them over to our teacher. She would know what was best to do—and if she

couldn't find out who the owner was she'd give them back to you. But you certainly ought to make enquiries before you eat them."

"Finding's keeping," said Bill again obstinately. "My mother says so."

"Then she's not much good as a mother if that's the kind of thing she teaches you," said George, beginning to lose his temper. "No wonder you tell fibs and cheat if that's the kind of mother you've got. No wonder you——"

"If you say another word I'll hit you!" shouted Bill—but just then the teacher came in and looked in surprise at the angry boys and the listening children.

"Didn't you hear the bell?" she said. "Come along

in at once—and take those scowls off your faces, Bill and George."

Bill put on an even bigger scowl when the teacher went out. He stuffed the little packet he had found into the satchel he had hung on his peg.

"I'll give you all a sweet at playtime," he said. "All except goody-goody George."

George turned away. He was sorry he had lost his temper now—and, after all, if Bill had the kind of mother who taught him wrong things he supposed Bill couldn't really help believing them. George felt glad his mother was different. You could always trust what she said.

At playtime Bill went to his satchel and got out the little packet. He ran into the playground with it.

"Come on—share them with me!" he cried. "There'll be two or three for everyone!"

George called to his little sister. "Sue! Don't you take one!"

"Of course I'm not going to," said Sue.

"Nor am I," said Ronnie. "I think the same as you, George."

"So do I," said Mark, and Fred and Connie said the same.

But Harry, Tom, Lennie, Joan and Betty came round Bill to share the sweets. Harry was greedy and took three. Bill was greedy, too, and he took three. The others had one each.

"They're not very nice, are they, when the first sweetness has been sucked off?" said Joan, and she spat hers out. "Funny sort of sweets. I don't like them."

Bill didn't like Joan spitting hers out, because it made George laugh. So he went on sucking his, but he swallowed them before he had quite finished them because they really did taste nasty.

Harry swallowed his, too, because he liked to do everything that Bill did. Tom, Lennie and Betty sucked theirs almost to the end, and then swallowed them quickly.

"I don't believe they are such nice sweets after all," said George with a laugh.

"Well, they are then," said Bill at once, and he took another sweet and popped it into his mouth. He handed the packet to Harry. Harry shook his head.

None of the others would take a sweet, either. Bill stuffed the packet into his pocket, and when he

thought no one was looking he spat out the last sweet he had in his mouth. It certainly wasn't nice after the first few sucks.

Everyone went in when the bell rang. It was a nice lesson that morning after playtime, one that everyone liked, because it was story-time. The teacher was reading the tales of Robin Hood, and they were very exciting.

The children settled down to listen. Miss Brown began reading.

Suddenly some of the children began to fidget. Miss Brown looked up with a frown. She glanced round the class of twelve children, and then she put down the book.

"Bill! Harry! Tom! What's the matter? Don't you feel well? You look so pale."

"I feel awful," said Bill, leaning his head on his hand. "Oh, Miss Brown, I do feel so ill. I want to be sick."

"George, take Bill outside," said Miss Brown. "Harry, do you feel sick, too?"

"I feel—funny," said Harry. "My head's funny. My throat's funny. Miss Brown, I want to be sick, too."

Then Tom gave a groan, and Lennie began to cry because he felt ill and frightened. Betty looked very white, and Joan held her head in her hands.

"What *is* the matter with you children?" said Miss Brown, in alarm. "Oh, Harry! Help him, somebody—he's fallen off his chair! Fred, help me to lay him flat on the floor. Put a cushion under his head. Oh dear, what *can* be the matter?"

"Shall I run across the road and get the doctor?" asked Ronnie. "I know he's in because I just saw his car."

"Yes, you'd better," said Miss Brown, really alarmed now, because certainly some of the children looked very ill indeed.

George came back into the classroom looking frightened. "Miss Brown! You must come to Bill. He's fainted or something."

Miss Brown fled out to poor Bill. Ronnie ran for the doctor. He was just going out again but he came straight across to the school when he heard the news that Ronnie panted out.

He carried Bill back into the classroom and laid him beside Harry. He looked quickly round the room, and saw how ill Lennie, Tom and Betty looked. Joan was white, too.

"What's happened?" he asked Miss Brown. "These children have been poisoned, Miss Brown. What have they been eating?"

"*Poisoned!*" said Miss Brown, amazed. "Oh dear! Children, what have you been eating?"

Neither Bill nor Harry could answer; they were far too ill. George answered instead.

"*I* know what it is—it's those sweets Bill found this morning! He had three or four, so did Harry. The others only had one—and Joan spat hers out. The rest of us wouldn't have them."

"What sweets? Quick, show me," said the doctor. George felt in Bill's pocket and brought out the little blue packet.

The doctor opened it and looked at the little yellow things inside. "Good gracious—what are we to do! These are pills—poisonous to young children! The chemist's boy must have dropped them on his delivery round this morning. Miss Brown, I must get these children into my car and take them straight to hospital. I'm afraid these two boys on the floor are very dangerously ill."

Sue and Connie began to cry. George helped the doctor to carry Bill and Harry to the car. They couldn't even walk. Tom, Lennie, Joan and Betty were helped along. They were all very, very frightened.

The doctor went off with them in his car. Miss Brown and the other children went back to the classroom. "We can't do any more lessons this

morning," she said in a shaky voice. "I must telephone to the mothers of those poor children. Oh, I hope they'll be all right. How *silly* to eat things like that! If only Bill had brought the packet to me, as he should have done, I could have told him at once they were pills and probably poisonous."

The children went home, solemn and scared. They poured out the story to their mothers, who looked very solemn, too. George's mother put her arms round George and Sue.

"Oh, George—Sue! I *am* glad you didn't take one of those sweets. Thank goodness you didn't."

"Well, you should thank yourself for that," said George. "You've always said that if we find anything we shouldn't keep it but try our best to find who lost it. And I was cross with Bill because he said 'Oh, finding's keeping'—and, of course, I wouldn't take one of the sweets, and neither would Sue. We remembered what you said."

"And Bill remembered what *his* mother said, and took the sweets for his own," said Sue. "His mother can't be very honest, Mummy—and so I suppose Bill isn't either."

"You mustn't say things like that," said her mother, though secretly she thought that Sue was perfectly right. "Poor Bill! I'm afraid he will be terribly ill."

He was. And so was Harry, because the two of them had eaten so many of the pills. Lennie and Tom and Betty had to stay in hospital for a day and night, and then they were better and went home. Joan wasn't very ill because she had been sensible enough to spit out her "sweet", and she went home that afternoon. But poor Bill and Harry are still in hospital, and are feeling very ill and miserable. George and Sue go to see them and take them books and flowers, and when the two boys see them coming in, their cheeks red and their eyes bright, they look at them with envy.

"I feel as if I shall never be right again!" says poor

Bill. "Oh, George—if only I'd believed you when you said 'Finding's *not* keeping!' I wouldn't have been the cause of making the others ill, too, then. I'll never do such a thing again, never! It was wrong as well as foolish."

"I wish somebody would write all this down so that other children would know what happened to us, and be warned," said Harry from his bed. "I'd like children everywhere to know. I would really."

Well, Harry was right, of course, and it was a good idea of his to want somebody to write their story. I thought I'd better do it—just in *case* there are still a few children who think that Finding is Keeping, and that they can eat anything they find.

Wasn't it a dreadful thing to happen?

Billy-Bob's Coconut

ONCE Billy-Bob and Belinda saw that a fair had come to their village. It was a fine fair, with all kinds of roundabouts and swings set up in the big field at the end of the village.

Mother said she would take Billy-Bob and Belinda. So they put on their hats and coats and scarves, and off they went to the fair.

"I shall have a ride on the roundabout," said Billy-Bob. "On that animal roundabout, I think. I shall choose a giraffe. Which animal will you choose, Belinda?"

"A duck," said Belinda. So they both got on the roundabout when it stopped. There was Billy-Bob high up on an enormous giraffe with a long neck, and there was Belinda on a small duck that wobbled from side to side as the music played. Round and round they went—it was great fun.

Then they wanted a slide on the slippery-slip. So they gave a man a penny, and he lent them a mat each to slide down on. They climbed up some steps, put their mats at the top of the slippery-slip, and then slid down it. Oh—what fun that was!

They did that again—and then they went on the roundabout again. Mother had given them each as much as twenty pence to spend, so they really did have a good time. At last Billy-Bob had only two pence left and Belinda had only one.

"When you've spent that, we must go home," said Mother. "It's nearly tea-time."

"I shall spend mine on having a throw at those coconuts," said Billy-Bob, who rather thought he would be a good shot. So he gave the girl one new penny and she handed him three wooden balls to throw at the coconuts at the back. He threw one hard. It missed. He threw another. It just touched a coconut.

"That was quite a good shot," said Mother. Billy-Bob aimed very carefully with his third ball. He threw it hard—and it a hit a coconut right off its stand. Billy-Bob was so pleased.

The girl picked it up and gave it to him. "Can I eat it when I get home and give Belinda some too?" asked Billy-Bob.

"I'm afraid not," said Mother. "Coconut isn't good for children. It gives them a pain."

"Oh, Mother! Then what can I do with my coconut? It will be wasted," said Billy-Bob sadly.

"Oh no, it won't," said Mother. "You can hang it outside your bedroom window, with a hole in each end, and the tits will simply love it. They will feast on it all the winter through, and be your friends."

"Oh, I really should like that," said Billy-Bob, pleased. "I'll hang up my coconut by my window."

"I'd like a coconut, too, to hang by *my* window,"

said Belinda at once.

"Well, you've got a penny left. Get some of those wooden balls to throw, and you may knock a coconut down as well," said Billy-Bob. So Belinda gave her last new penny to the girl, and took the three balls. But, you know, she threw very badly indeed.

The first ball hit poor Billy-Bob on the back! It didn't really hurt him very much, but he felt rather angry.

"Can't you see the difference between me and the coconuts?" he said to Belinda. Belinda frowned, and threw her second ball. This time it hit the girl who gave out the balls!

"Really, Belinda!" said Mother. "You must *look* where you are throwing! Now do be careful of your last ball."

"*I*'m going to get out of the way," said Billy-Bob, and he stood yards away. Belinda threw the ball. It went high into the air, and dropped down nearly on top of her own head.

"You're a dreadful thrower!" said Billy-Bob in disgust, "A waste of money, I call that."

"I haven't got a coconut," wailed Belinda. "I want some more money."

"Well, you can't have any more, Belinda," said Mother firmly. "Firstly, because you're acting like a baby and you know I never give you anything then. Secondly, because you've used up all your money. And thirdly, because I've none left in my purse, anyhow."

Billy-Bob felt sorry for Belinda. "Look, Belinda," he said. "I'll spend my last new pence on some more balls and *I'll* throw them and get you a coconut to take home."

So he paid for the three balls and aimed very carefully. But not one of them hit a coconut at all. Billy-Bob was very sorry.

"Now we *must* go home," said Mother. "Didn't we have a lovely time? Cheer up, Belinda. The world isn't coming to an end because you haven't got a coconut!"

So Belinda cheered up; but when they got home and Mother knocked a hole in each end of the coconut and then threaded string through the holes to hang the

nut up by Billy-Bob's window, Belinda was very sad.

"I want some birds at my window too," she said. "I don't see why Billy-Bob should have all the birds. I love them too."

Well, the birds *did* come to Billy-Bob's coconut. They came all day long! There were great-tits with black heads and bright green and yellow feathers, and blue-tits with blue caps and shrill high voices. It was such fun to watch them.

"I do wish I could have the birds at my window," said Belinda a dozen times a day to Billy-Bob and Mother. And then one day Mother said something exciting.

"Belinda, if you really want birds by your window, you have something in your own garden that they will love to eat if you hang it up on string."

"Oh, Mother, what?" cried Belinda.

"Come and see," said Mother. She and Belinda went down the garden and Mother pointed to the big old heads of Belinda's giant sunflowers. "Look," said Mother. "Those old sunflowers of yours have made heaps of seeds in their big fat middles. The finches and the sparrows love those. Shall we cut one down and hang it up for you?"

"Oh yes!" cried Belinda joyfully. So they cut the biggest one down, and Mother put some string round it and hung it up by Belinda's window.

And now *Belinda* has birds all day long at her window too—not the same ones as Billy-Bob, but sparrows and chaffinches and greenfinches, and sometimes a shy bullfinch with its black velvet head and deep red chest. Oh, Belinda has plenty of bird-friends now!

Can you get a coconut or an old giant sunflower head? If you can, hang one by *your* window! You'll have just as much fun then as Billy-Bob and Belinda do!

A Hole in Her Stocking

MOLLIE was ten years old, so she was a big girl. She was supposed to make her own bed, to dust her own room, to mend her clothes and to darn her stockings.

But Mollie was lazy. She often pulled her bed together instead of making it properly. She sometimes flicked the duster over her room instead of dusting in every corner. She often used safety-pins to pin her frock together when a button was off, and if a hole in her stocking didn't show she wouldn't darn it!

Mollie lived with her aunt and her three cousins in a country village. Her father and mother were away at work, and she had quite a nice time with her cousins. There was Oliver, the boy, and Jane and Fanny, the two girls. Mollie and the two girls slept together in a big bedroom that had three little beds in it.

Christmas-time was coming, and the children wondered what presents they would get. What fun to wake up on Christmas morning and see their stockings full! How lovely to see what was in them, right down to the toes!

When Christmas Eve came they could *not* go to sleep. Mollie's aunt saw them into bed and told them to hang up their longest stockings.

"And we'll hope they will be full in the morning" she said.

Mollie looked in her stocking drawer. She pulled out a long, black stocking. It had a big hole in the toe, but she hadn't bothered to mend it, because it didn't show when she wore her shoe on her foot. She took out the stocking and hung it at the head of the bed, twisting it round the knob.

"My stocking's ready!" she said.

"So are ours!" said the others. They all got into bed and tried to go to sleep. But they talked and laughed such a lot that it was quite impossible to sleep. Mollie's aunt came in at last and spoke quite sternly. "If I hear one more word I shall take down your stockings and put them back into the drawer!"

After that there wasn't even a whisper. It would have been too dreadful to have no stocking on Christmas morning!

Now that night all the stockings were filled. Shall I tell you what went into Mollie's stocking? Well, first of all, a bright ten pence piece. It fell down the stocking—right to the toe—and, alas, because there was a hole there, it dropped out of the toe on to the carpet and rolled under the bed! The next thing put in was a dear little red ball—and that dropped out of the big hole and rolled away to a corner of the room!

A HOLE IN HER STOCKING

Then a stick of barley-sugar, wrapped in bright paper, slipped into the stocking—and out of the toe! Next came a blue pencil and a little square rubber. Both of them dropped down to the toe—and out of the hole. They fell to the floor and bounced away.

Then a little red apple was put in—and that almost *did* stay in the stocking, for it was nearly as big as the hole. But it hung for a moment over the hole and then dropped with a soft bounce on to the floor, where it rolled off under the chest-of-drawers.

Then came a tiny doll, dressed like a sailor, and he fell out of the hole almost as soon as he was put in the stocking! Last of all there was a bar of chocolate, and that fell out, too. So by the time that the other children's stockings were filled to the top poor Mollie's was quite empty!

In the morning Jane awoke first. She gave a squeal at the sight of her bulging stocking and sat up at once. Fanny awoke and squealed, too.

"Mollie! Wake up! It's Christmas morning!" cried Fanny. "Our stockings are full. Oh, I've got *such* a dear little doll!"

"And I've got a duck to float in the bath!" said Jane. There was a yell from the other room.

"Hey, you girls! Come and look what I've got! I've got a clown who turns head-over-heels!"

This sounded so exciting that Jane and Fanny picked up their stockings and rushed into Oliver's room to see his clown.

Mollie sat up, excited. She looked at the stocking at the head of her bed. It didn't look very fat. She

put out her hand to feel it. If didn't *feel* fat, either! She pulled it towards her. She put her hand in—right the way down—and there was nothing, nothing, nothing in it at all!

The little girl's heart sank. Why was there nothing in it? What had happened? Was there a present on her bed, perhaps? No, there was nothing there either. There was no present from anyone.

"They don't like me," she thought, and the tears came into her eyes. "They don't think I'm a nice little girl. No one has given me anything!"

She dressed quickly and slipped downstairs. She hid behind the big curtains at the sitting-room window

"Where's Mollie?" asked Jane, in a surprised voice, when everyone was sitting at breakfast. "I haven't seen her since we went into Oliver's room this morning."

"There she is—behind the curtain!" said Oliver suddenly. "She's crying! Mollie, what's the matter?"

"There was n-n-n-nothing in my st-st-stocking!" wept Mollie. "I hadn't any presents at all. Nobody loves me!"

"But, darling, of course we all love you!" said her aunt in surprise. "You've made a mistake, Mollie—your stocking is full! I expect you took the wrong stocking! Go upstairs and get it. Bring it down here and you'll see how full it is!"

Mollie went upstairs. She took the empty stocking and sadly brought it down to show everyone. Oliver put his hand right down to the toe—and his fingers came waggling out of the end!

He gave a shout of laughter. "Mollie! You chose a stocking with a big, big hole in it, you silly! You chose one you put away without darning, naughty girl! All your presents must have dropped out! They will be on the floor!"

Everyone rushed upstairs to look—and, sure enough, there was the ten pence piece on the floor under the bed—and there was the ball—and the barley-sugar—and the doll—and the chocolate—and everything. All on the floor. Mollie didn't know whether to laugh or to cry.

"Oh dear!" she said. "Oh dear! How silly I am! And, oh, I do feel ashamed of that big hole I didn't darn! Oh, Auntie, I'm so sorry. I know I should mend the holes in my stockings—and haven't I been well punished for forgetting!"

"Never mind, dear," said her aunt. "Everything is all right now. You've got a fine lot of presents and Christmas is going to be lovely!"

So it was—and I expect you know what one of Mollie's New Year Resolutions was, don't you? Yes—to be sure and darn every hole in her stockings.

It Happened One Afternoon

MIKE WENT whistling into his father's study to borrow a map. He and his friend Jo were going on a week-end bicycle tour, and Mike wanted to work out the best way to go.

Mike felt happy. It was a wonderful day, and looked like being a wonderful week-end. He and Jo were to go off that evening, after Jo had finished up at the office he worked at. He was fifteen, and very anxious to get on. Mike was almost fourteen and still at school.

It was half-term. His bicycle was cleaned, ready for the week-end. His mother had already packed him up a bag of food. His father had given him a pound to spend on himself and Jo over the week-end. Everything was fine.

He found the map and slipped it into his pocket. Then he caught sight of a new golf club that his father had bought himself. It stood by the table, neat and shining.

"Ha! Dad's got a new club!" said Mike, and he picked it up. "I bet I could hit a golf ball as far as he can! Wheeeeeee!"

He swung it up behind him and brought it down. CRASH!

Mike turned in fright. He had smashed a lamp and a very valuable vase. There they lay on the floor in hundreds of pieces.

Mike did the first thing he thought of. He shot out of the room, down the passage to the garden door and out to the shed. He hid there, trembling.

"Dad would be furious if he thought I'd done that," he thought. "So would Mother. They wouldn't let me go away for the week-end with Jo. I wouldn't be surprised if Dad gave me a good hiding."

He stayed there for a long while. He could hear excited voices, and knew that the breakages had been discovered. He wondered what to do.

He didn't think of owning up, and facing up to his punishment. Let them think it was the cat! Tabs was always breaking something.

He stayed in the shed till tea-time. He knew his mother would have gone out by then to see his grandmother. Dad didn't seem to be about either—maybe he had gone for a walk. He wouldn't bother about tea. He would just scribble a note to say he was sorry they were out when he set off for his week-end.

"I don't want to face them so soon after the things got broken," he thought. "I'll just let them think I couldn't say good-bye because they weren't here when I left—and by Monday perhaps they'll have forgotten all about the accident, and won't ask any awkward questions."

He scribbled his note, crept out and snooped around to see where everyone was.

"No sign of Mother, and no sign of Dad either," he thought. "Good. I'll leave the note on Mother's chair. She'll see it when she comes back."

He left the note, jumped on his bicycle and rode off down the path and into the lane to go to Jo's. His kit-bag was on his shoulder, with the things in it he would need. Jo was bringing some, too. It would be fun!

He rode in at the gate at the bottom of Jo's garden. He gave the whistle that he and Jo used—but Jo didn't seem to be there.

"Blow! There's his bike, all ready—where on earth is Jo?"

He heard a movement in the little summer-house nearby, and then a scared and anxious face looked out at him. It was Jo's sister, twelve-year-old Jane.

"Jane! What's the matter?" asked Mike at once. "You're crying. What's happened? Is somebody ill?"

"No," said Jane, with a gulp. "Oh, Mike! It's awful!"

"What's awful?" said Mike, going into the summer-house, feeling very worried. He was fond of Jane. "Have you gone and got yourself into trouble, Jane? What have you done? Lost your homework again?"

"No, Mike—nothing like that. It's poor Jo," said Jane, and began to cry again.

"What's happened to him?" asked Mike, impatiently. "He ought to be here, ready to start out with me. Don't say something's happened to stop him!"

"He's not coming," said Jane, almost in a whisper. "He's in awful trouble. He's lost his job at Mr. Frost's office. Dad's furious with him."

"Gosh—but what's he *done*?" asked Mike. "Do tell me, Jane. This is awful."

"I don't know exactly what he's done, nor where it all happened," said Jane. "They wouldn't let me be in the room. All I know is that Jo was sent out to deliver some important papers from the office this afternoon—and—and they say he went to deliver them—climbed in at the window, because he saw a gold watch there—and stole it!"

Mike listened, absolutely amazed. *Jo!* Why, Jo was as honest as the day. "It can't be true," he said at last. "It's a wicked thing to say about Jo!"

"Yes, I know," said Jane, wiping away her tears. "But he was found standing in the room—and the watch was gone. They think he must have thrown it out of the window as soon as he heard someone coming. That's what they *say*."

"But they must be *mad*," said Mike. "Jo *couldn't* do a thing like that! He simply couldn't. He must have been in the room for some quite good reason. I know Jo!"

"Jo said he heard a peculiar noise and jumped in to see what it was," said Jane. "They didn't believe him, of course."

"Look here!" said Mike, feeling very fierce all of a sudden. "I'm going to find out where this place is that Jo's supposed to have stolen the watch from. I'm going to go and *see* these horrible people there. I'm

going to tell them that Jo's my friend and couldn't do a mean thing to save his life! See, Jane?"

"Oh, Mike!" said Jane, looking at him with the greatest admiration. "Would you really be brave enough to do all that? You *would* be a good friend to Jo!"

"He's my best friend—and I won't let anyone treat him like that or say things like that about him!" said Mike. "What's more, when I've seen these people and told them what I think of them, I shall go and see your father and mother, and tell them they ought to know better than to think old Jo would ever do such a thing as steal a gold watch, and tell lies about it!"

He got up and Jane got up, too, drying her eyes. "Perhaps they'll let you and Jo go off for the week-end after all," she said. "Oh, Mike—I do think you are wonderful."

"Where's Jo?" said Mike. "Come on—let's find him."

Jo was in his room, sulky and miserable. Mike went up to him and banged him on the back.

"Cheer up, old chap! I'll go and face these people who say things like that about you! Tell me all about it."

"Haven't you *heard* all about it?" asked Jo, looking suddenly astonished.

"Well—only what Jane's told me," said Mike. Jo went on looking astonished, and didn't say a word. "Do tell me what happened," said Mike. "I want to know so that I can march straight off to these people and tell them what I think of them."

Jo looked at Mike doubtfully. "Well—it seems odd

that you haven't heard all about it yet," he said. "I'll tell you exactly what happened. I was told to take some important papers to a client this afternoon. So off I went. Well, as I passed a window as I was walking up to the front door, I suddenly heard a most terrific *crash*! I nearly jumped out of my skin. I looked in at the open window and saw a frightful mess on the floor."

"What was it?" asked Mike.

"I don't really know," said Jo. "Anyway, I stood there wondering what had caused all the noise and mess and thought I'd better investigate. So I jumped in at the wondow—but I hadn't been there more than a moment before in came the household, and shouted at me to know what I was doing there, and what had I smashed!"

"Go on," said Mike. "What beastly people!"

"I was just explaining that I'd jumped in merely to see what was happening when somebody called out that a gold watch was missing—it had been left on the table—and it wasn't there. So they thought *I'd* taken it—got in at the window, you see, knocked over heaps of things, and then got frightened and chucked the watch away."

"I call this all absolute rubbish!" said Mike, fiercely. "If they knew you they'd never say things like that about you, Jo."

"Actually, they *did* know me," said Jo. "But it didn't make any difference. They rang up Mr. Frost, and told him what they thought I'd done, and when I got back to the office, he was very angry at my behaviour and sacked me—gave me my money and sent me off straight away. My father's furious."

"I'm going to see these hateful people," said Mike. "Who are they? Tell me their name and address, Jo."

Jo didn't say anything. He went very red and looked at the floor.

"Go on, Jo—tell me quickly," said Mike.

"Mike," said Jo, in a low voice, "it—it was *your* house and *your* family. You see, I thought I knew you well enough to leap in at the window to see if anything was going wrong—I didn't realise they'd think I'd smashed those things, and taken the watch."

Mike sat down suddenly. He stared at Jo. A horrid sick feeling came over him, and thoughts raced through his mind. He knew in a trice what had happened!

Jo had just been passing his house when he, Mike, had smashed the vase and the lamp with his father's golf club. Jo had leapt in to see what the noise was—and had found nobody there, because Mike had run straight out of the room and hidden. The gold watch? Yes, it had been there all right—but probably Mike had hit that, too, and quite likely it was in some dark corner of the room, smashed to bits.

He sat staring at Jo, feeling wicked and very miserable. Jo had been punished for something he, Mike, had done and had run away from. Jo had lost his job. Jo was in disgrace. Their week-end was ruined. What was to be done?

"You see—you won't go and face those people now," said Jo, miserably. "They're your own people. They wouldn't believe even *you*!"

Mike stood up, very pale. "They *will* believe me," he said. "And you'll get your job back, and your father will be very sorry he scolded you. You'll see! But we shan't go off for our week-end. And shall I tell you why? It's because you'll never want to see me again after to-day!"

He went off, leaving Jane and Jo very surprised and puzzled. He knew what he had to do. He had to do the thing he had run away from that afternoon. He had to go and own up and take his punishment.

He went straight home and found his father. "Dad," he said, "ring up Mr. Frost and tell him to take Jo back at once. *I'm* the one to blame."

"Now, what exactly do you mean, Mike?" said his father, astonished.

Mike told him. "I came in here and saw your new golf club. I swung it—and smashed the lamp and the vase. And I was a coward and ran off to hide in the shed. I hoped Mother would think it was the cat who had broken the things. I didn't know Jo was going to be blamed."

His father listened in silence, his face very grave. "What about the gold watch?" he said. "That's missing, as you know."

"It's probably lying in the grate, or under the bookcase, smashed," said Mike. "I may have hit that too and sent it flying. I'll look, Dad."

He looked—and sure enough the watch was under the bookcase, badly damaged. He laid it in front of his father in silence.

"Punish me twice," said Mike. "Once for doing all

this and once for making the blame fall on someone else. I know I'm a coward and you're ashamed of me. I'm ashamed of myself. I've lost your good opinion, and I shall have lost Mother's trust—and I've certainly lost Jo's friendship. I'm a—a worm."

"Yes. I rather think you are," said his father. "The only good thing in the whole affair is that you owned up when you saw that Jo was being punished. I'm disappointed in you. Horribly disappointed. It will take you a long while to get back my trust and make me proud of you—and your Mother will think the same. Now go away and ask your Mother to come to me."

Mike was in for a very bad time indeed. His father would hardly speak to him. His mother looked as if she was going to burst into tears each time she looked at him. Mr. Frost turned the other way when he met him.

But would you believe it, *Jo* didn't turn against him! He was just the same as usual, friendly, kind and generous.

"Ass!" he said, when Mike thanked him for being so decent. "Aren't I your friend? You're in trouble and you want help. All right, that's what a friend is for. Come on, we'll face this together, and when everyone sees us about as usual, they'll soon forget what's happened! You *were* a coward—but you were jolly brave, too, to go and own up just for me!"

Things will work out all right, of course, but what a good thing for Mike that he had a friend like Jo! I'd like to be as good a friend as that, wouldn't you?

The Little Lost Hen

One afternoon, when Harry was coming home from school, he saw a little red hen. That doesn't sound very surprising, but when I tell you that the hen was just about to cross the road in the busy street, all by itself, you will see why Harry was rather astonished.

"Goodness!" said Harry, in surprise. "What is that hen doing in the middle of the town all by itself? It will get run over if it tries to cross this busy street. It must have escaped from somewhere and got lost."

A car hooted at the hen and it ran back to the kerb, fluttering its red feathers and squawking loudly. Harry was worried. What was he to do? You couldn't tell a hen to go home, as you could tell a dog.

"There's nothing to be done but to pick up the hen and take it home with me," thought Harry. "I can put it into my nursery until I know who the owner is."

Now Harry wasn't very good at picking up birds. Some people love picking up anything, and don't mind touching worms or spiders. It is good to be like

that, but Harry wasn't. He shivered when he tried to pick up the hen. He didn't like it at all.

The hen was so frightened that she let herself be picked up without struggling a bit. Harry managed to get her under his left arm, and held her there with his right hand. She tried to peck him and he nearly dropped her. But he just managed to hold on, and off he went home, with the hen under his arm.

When he got home he called for his mother, but she was out. Jane, the maid, was in the garden hanging out some tea-cloths. So Harry went into the house by himself, carrying the little lost hen.

He went to his nursery and looked round. Where could he put the hen to make her comfortable? He saw his barrow there, and he carefully put the hen into it.

But she was out at once and ran clucking all round the nursery in a great way because she didn't know where she was.

"Oh, Hen, don't be so silly," said Harry. "Are you hungry? Stop pecking at my soldiers, please!"

Harry went out and shut the door. He went to the cupboard where Mother kept the seed for her pigeons and got a handful from a bag. Then back he went to the nursery.

"Kuk-kuk-kuk-kuk-kuk!" said the hen, running to Harry.

"Kuk-kuk," answered the boy, and threw a handful of seed on the carpet. The hen pecked it up greedily. Then she cocked her bright-eyed head on one side and looked at Harry.

"Kuk-kuk-kuk!" she said in a very kindly tone.

Harry didn't understand what she said, but what she meant was that she thought he was a very kind little boy. She began to peck up the rest of the seed.

Then Harry heard his mother's voice and he flew downstairs to tell her about the little lost hen. But Mother had a visitor with her, and Harry had to be quiet and not say a word except how-do-you-do. Mother wouldn't let him talk when visitors were there, unless he was spoken to.

But after a while Mother heard a peculiar noise from the nursery, and she frowned.

"I wonder what that funny noise upstairs is," she said. "It's very queer!"

Everybody listened—and they could hear the hen clucking loudly. Then sudden she cackled at the top of her voice!

"Cackle-cackle-cackle, cluck, cluck, cluck!"

"It sounds like a hen!" said Mother in astonishment. "Well, I never!"

"It *is* a hen!" said Harry, and he told his mother all about the little hen he had found trying to cross the street.

"Harry! Do you really mean to say that you put the hen in the nursery!" said Mother. "Oh, whatever will you do next!"

"It must be Mrs. White's hen," said the visitor, Miss Brown. "She told me this morning that her favourite red hen had escaped, and she didn't know where it had gone!"

"Oh, then, do you mind taking it back to her?" cried Harry. "The poor little hen feels so strange in my nursery. It would be so pleased to go back home again to all its friends."

"Of course I will," said Miss Brown, and they all went upstairs. There was the hen, scratching at the carpet, and clucking softly to itself. It ran to Harry and pecked at a freckle on his legs. Miss Brown picked it up.

"Would you like a basket to take it home in?" asked Harry's mother.

"Oh no. I like the nice soft warm feel of a hen," said Miss Brown, cuddling the little red hen to her. "My word, won't Mrs. White be pleased when she sees me walking in with her lost hen! It is her very favourite one, and lays her a big brown egg every day."

"I love brown eggs," said Harry. "They taste much nicer than white ones. I wish I had a hen that laid me brown eggs."

"We haven't room in our garden to keep hens," said Mother. "Well, good-bye, Miss Brown, and I do hope the hen will behave itself and not try to get out of your arms!"

Miss Brown and the hen went away. Harry felt quite lonely without the little red hen in his nursery. He wandered round by himself, wondering what to play with. He thought he would play with the soldiers in his toy fort.

So he went over to the fort—but before he could pick up any of his soldiers he saw something that made him stare and stare!

In the very middle of his toy fort was a big brown

egg! Yes—there it lay among the soldiers, big and brown and smooth. Harry gave a scream of joy and picked it up. It was warm—as warm as toast!

"Mother! Mother! Come and look here!" yelled Harry. "Oh, quick, do come!"

Mother came rushing in—and when she saw the egg she laughed and laughed.

"Well, really, Harry, this is the funniest thing I ever heard of! You find a hen and bring it to your nursery and feed it—and it lays an egg in your toy fort! I will ring up Mrs. White and tell her, and you can take the egg round to her in a basket."

So Mother rang up Mrs. White and told her. When she put down the telephone she turned to Harry.

"Mrs. White says that the hen must have meant the egg for *you*, Harry, in return for your kindness," said Mother. "She says you are to keep it and eat it for breakfast!"

"Oh, Mother! What a surprise! And I do so like brown eggs!" said Harry in delight. "How kind of the hen to think of me like that!"

So Harry had the brown egg for his breakfast, and he told me that it was the very nicest one he had ever had in his life. Wasn't he lucky?

The Silly Storyteller

I WONDER if you have ever met Percival Jonathan Jenks? He is a small boy with brown hair, grey eyes, and plenty of brown freckles all over his face and hands. He went to school with all the other children, and as he was generous with his sweets and toys they liked him.

But there was one curious thing about Percival, and that was that he did make up the silliest stories!

"I call them untruths," said Jane.

"They are more like pretends," said Mary.

"They're jolly silly, anyhow," said Jack.

"In class at school to-day, when our teacher was telling us about Canada, Percival put up his hand and said he had been there—and he hasn't!" said Harry.

"And yesterday when we passed the fireworks shop, Percival said he had bought twenty pence worth of rockets and I know he hadn't, because I asked his Mother," said Ann.

"And this morning Percival told me he had seen a parrot in the school garden and it said, 'Hallo, Percival,' to him!" said Jane. "It's wrong to tell stories like that. I don't like story tellers."

"The funny thing is," said Mary, "that Percival himself really seems to believe what he is saying! Do you think he knows the difference between what is true and what isn't?"

"My Mother says some children don't, and they have to be taught," said Jack. "She says it's no good punishing them, because that only makes them worse and they tell more stories than ever. She says they have to be taught the difference between telling silly pretended stories and the real truth."

"Well, let's teach Percival then!" said Jane, with a giggle. "It's time he learnt! He sent me all the way down the school playground yesterday to see an escaped monkey in a tree—and of course there wasn't one!"

"Yes—let's teach him," said Harry. "One of these days he'll get into serious trouble if he doesn't soon learn to be sensible."

"How shall we teach him?" asked Ann.

"By telling him just the same sort of silly things as he tells us!" said Jack. "He'll soon get tired of believing our silly stories, and when we tell him they're the same as his, maybe he'll get tired of his too!"

"Right! We'll begin to-day!" said Harry. They all laughed. Poor Percival! They were going to have some fun with him!

That afternoon the children all went back to school early to play. Percival went too. Ann ran up to him.

"Percival," she said, "have you seen the red cat in the garden shed over there? It's most extraordinary!"

"A red cat!" said Percival in surprise. "Oooh, I

must go and see it! I've never seen a red cat before."

He ran off to the shed. The other children giggled and watched him. Percival looked all round the shed. He hunted everywhere. There was no red cat to be found, of course. He went back to Ann, very angry.

"There's no cat there," he said. "You told me a story, Ann!"

"Well, it was just about as true as that escaped monkey you sent Jane to see!" said Ann. Then the school bell rang, and they all went in.

After school Harry ran up to Percival. "I spent five pence on sweets to-day," he said. "I got peppermints and toffees and caramels."

"Have you eaten them all?" asked Percival eagerly. "Let me walk home with you, Harry."

"You can if you like," said Harry, laughing, as he

saw the other children smiling around him. "I haven't eaten any of the sweets at all. You can share them."

So Percival walked home with Harry—but Harry didn't offer him any sweets.

"What about those peppermints and caramels and toffees?" Percival said at last. "Can't I have a few, Harry?"

"Oh yes," said Harry. "Put your hand in my pockets and get as many as you like."

So Percival felt in all Harry's pockets—but of course there were no sweets there at all! Harry laughed at Percival's cross face.

"Did you really suppose I would ever have five

pence to spend on sweets?" he said. "My sweets were the same as those fireworks you told us you bought the other day—not real at all."

Percival was very angry. He didn't say another word but ran off home by himself. Harry told the other children about it the next day, and they laughed.

When Jane saw Percival coming to school she called him. "Percival! Your dog has run into the classroom. Hadn't you better send him home?"

Percival ran at once into school and hunted for his dog. But of course it wasn't there. He came out, red and angry.

"You told a story, Jane," he said.

"Of course I did!" said Jane. "Just like the story you told one day of a cat in somebody's desk, and there wasn't! Ha, ha!"

John went up to Percival and spoke to him. "I'm having a party this afternoon," he said. "Would you like to come?"

"Oh yes!" said Percival, pleased. "I'll run home and change into my party-things after afternoon school and come then."

But in a little while he heard Harry say that John was going to tea with *him* that day. So there couldn't be a party at John's house!

Percival was angry and scolded John. "Why did you say you were going to have a party to-day?" he said. "It wasn't true."

"Well, last week you said you were going to go to the Zoo and you asked Jane, and then we found you weren't going after all," said John.

Percival glared at John. "There seems to be a lot of make-up all of a sudden," he said.

"There does, doesn't there?" said John. "We must have caught it from you!"

Before Percival could say any more, Mary danced up. "Percival, I saw a big hedgehog in your garden as I went past to-day. Aren't you lucky?"

"Did you really?" said Percival. "I'll look for it when I get home."

He did. He spent an hour hunting for that hedgehog, but of course it wasn't there. He was very vexed with Mary the next day.

"You made that hedgehog up," he said. "It wasn't real."

"Oh no, it wasn't real," said Mary. "It was the same kind of creature as that parrot you said you saw in the garden the other day. We are quite enjoying making up silly stories to trick you, Percival."

"But there's a difference between *our* pretends and yours," said Jack.

"What difference is there?" said Percival sulkily.

"Well, we do know when we are making up stories and when we are not," said Jack. "We do know what is real and what isn't. You don't."

Percival stared at Jack. "I see what you mean," he said, turning red. "Yes—I know I sometimes make up things that aren't true. But now that you've begun to do the same, I can quite well see the difference—and I don't like it. Jack, please stop. It's horrid."

"Well, will you stop, if we do?" asked Jack.

"I'll try to," said Percival. "I've rather got into the habit of being silly over make-ups, but if you'll all help me, I'll soon get out of it."

The children crowded round Percival, who looked very serious. "Don't look so miserable," said Jane. "We only did it for a bit of fun. We didn't think you were really untruthful, you know—only rather silly because you didn't seem to know what was real and what wasn't!"

"I do, if I think about it," said Percival, cheering up. "Now don't you tell me any more stories, any of you, will you? I want to be able to trust you again!"

"Right!" said Jack. "We'll trust you, and you can trust us! No more silly make-ups from anybody, please!"

You will hardly believe it, but Percival didn't tell a single silly story from that day. He saw very plainly how stupid it was when the others did it to him. I think they were rather clever to cure him in such a simple way, don't you?

Derek's Motor-car

DEREK had a motor-car. It was just big enough for himself, and he loved it very much. It was bright red, and had two lamps in front and a red one behind. But, what a pity, it hadn't a hooter!

Derek was always wishing it had. He said so quite twenty times a day, and really, Mummy got quite tired of hearing it.

"Derek, hooters cost about ten pence," she said, "and I haven't got ten pence to spare. Now run away, there's a good boy, and don't worry me any more."

"Well, Mummy, I don't know what to *do*!" said Derek. "You see, I've got my car to drive about in, but there's nowhere to *go*. You won't let me go for a long drive into the country."

"I should think not!" said Mummy. "You may go as far as the shops and back and that's all. Now, go along, and don't let me hear another grumble about that hooter, *please!*"

Derek opened the red door of his car, climbed in, sat down on the seat, and shut the door. It had a little handle that shut the door properly, just like a real car. It was really lovely. But it *was* a pity it hadn't a hooter!

"Suppose I ran into somebody and there was an accident!" said Derek to himself. "If I can't hoot,

how can I tell people to get out of the way? Really, I do *wish* I had a hooter. I wish Mummy would buy me one."

He pedalled off down the path. He went out of the gate and very soon he met Harry, the boy over the road.

"Hallo," said Harry. "I do like your car."

"Yes, but it hasn't got a hooter," said Derek. "Isn't it a pity?"

"Well, why don't you get one?" asked Harry.

"Mummy hasn't the money to buy me one," said Derek.

"Well, good gracious, can't you get the hooter yourself?" said Harry. "My Mummy says that if you want a thing badly enough you can always find a way to get it!"

And he went off down the road, whistling. Derek stared after him, thinking hard.

"Well!" he thought. "That's an idea! Why should I expect other people to get me the things I want? Why shouldn't I try to get them myself? I could perhaps earn some money to buy the hooter!"

So he pedalled off to Mrs. Jones, who had once given him two pence for running an errand. She was at the garden gate, looking for Dick, her big boy.

"Hallo, Derek," she said. "Have you seen Dick? I want him to go down to the chemist for me."

"No, I haven't seen him," said Derek. "But I'll go for you, Mrs. Jones."

He didn't say anything about his hooter, or how he hoped Mrs. Jones might give him two pence. Mummy had always told him he must do things for nothing, and then, if people *were* kind enough to give him a penny, well, that was a nice surprise!

"Oh, thank you," said Mrs. Jones. "It won't take you long in that nice car of yours. Run along and ask them to give you a pound of cotton-wool for Mrs. Jones."

So off went Derek, pedalling away fast. He came to the chemist shop and parked his car outside. He went in and asked for the cotton-wool. He took the big packet out and put it on the seat beside the wheel. There was just room for it. Back he pedalled to Mrs. Jones.

"Good boy!" she said. "You've been quick! Here is two pence!"

"Oh, thank you, Mrs. Jones," said Derek, pleased, and he put it into his pocket. The first two pence! Then he pedalled away again, wondering how he could earn his next penny.

He met old Mrs. Lacy, and she had so many parcels that she really didn't know how to carry them all. Derek pedalled up to her.

"Mrs. Lacy! Put your parcels into my car and I'll carry them for you," he said. Mrs. Lacy looked down, very pleased indeed.

"Kind child!" she said, and she put her parcels into the little motor-car. Derek pedalled proudly in front of her with them, all the way home. Then he handed her out the parcels.

"I wonder if you'd like an orange in return for your kindness, or a penny to spend?" said Mrs. Lacy, smiling at him.

"Well, I don't mind having nothing at all, if you can't afford it," said Derek, remembering that Mrs. Lacy was poor. "But if you can, why, I'd love to have a penny. You see, I'm saving up for a new hooter."

"Ah! Then you certainly must have the penny," said Mrs. Lacy, and she handed one to him. Derek said thank you and put it into his pocket. Three pence already!

"If you pedal down to my sister, Mrs. White, maybe she will have a job for you too," said Mrs. Lacy. "I know she is very busy this morning."

So Derek pedalled off to the little old cottage where Mrs. White lived. She was taking the eggs out of her hen-house and counting them.

"Good morning, Mrs. White," said Derek politely, raising his cap. "Mrs. Lacy told me to come and see if there was anything I could do for you."

"You're just the person I want!" said Mrs. White. "Can you take a basket of eggs to Miss Brown, do you think—and then come back again and take two dozen to Mr. Thomas over the hill? My leg is bad this morning and I really can't walk all that way."

"Oh yes, certainly," said Derek, and he took the basket at once. He pedalled away to Miss Brown's—and, do you know, wasn't it surprising, she gave him a penny for bringing the eggs! That really *was* a surprise to Derek!

"Now I've got four pence!" he said, and he went back to Mrs. White's for the other eggs. He took them to Mr. Thomas, but he didn't get any penny there, for Mr. Thomas was not a very kind old man.

He took a third lot of eggs to the dairy as well, and when he went back to tell Mrs. White he had done that and was there anything else, she said no—and gave him two pence!

"You're a kind little chap," she said. "You deserve a reward."

"But Miss Brown gave me a penny when I left her eggs," said Derek. "You should only give me one penny, Mrs. White, because I've already got one for the eggs."

But Mrs. White made him have two—so now he had six! He was getting rich. He pedalled to the toy-shop to see how much a hooter was, and he found that he could get a beautiful one for nine pence, a really good one that would hoot like a proper car—not a silly little pip-pip one like Eileen had on her bicycle.

On the way home Derek had a real piece of luck. Whatever do you suppose it was? He *found* a penny lying on the path! Think of that! Nobody was about so he couldn't ask anyone if they had dropped it. He got out of his car and picked up the penny. Now he had seven pence!

"It's time for dinner," said Derek. "I'm hungry. Perhaps this afternoon I can earn some more money. Oh, this is better than asking other people to buy me things! I feel much prouder when I'm doing it all myself."

Now, when he was sitting down to dinner, Mother suddenly said, "Oh, it's your cousin Robert's birthday to-morrow, Derek. You should buy him a present. Have you any pennies in your money-box?"

"No, Mummy," said Derek. "I took them all out to buy Daddy a new pipe for *his* birthday."

Derek went rather red when he said this, for he knew quite well he had seven pence in his pocket. He didn't say a word about them. Oh, he really, couldn't spend them on Robert, when he had worked so hard to get them to buy a new hooter.

"Poor Robert is ill," said Mummy, giving Derek some pudding. "It will be so nice for him to have a few presents to-morrow. He can't even have a piece of his birthday-cake, poor boy, and no party at all."

Derek listened, and felt his pennies. He was sorry for Robert. It was dreadful, really dreadful, not to be

able to eat birthday-cake on a birthday. Suddenly he made up his mind. He would spend his seven pennies on Robert!

"Mummy, I earned seven pence this morning by going errands," he said. "I meant to save them up to buy a hooter, but I'll buy Robert something instead."

"That's very generous of you, Derek," said Mummy. "I'm proud of you."

Derek was pleased to hear his mother say that. He did like her to be proud of him. He went out in the afternoon and spent a long time in the toy-shop, choosing something for Robert. At last he bought a two penny top, a penny book, and a four penny motor-car. He thought Robert would rather have three things than one if he were ill.

But he didn't look at the hooters at all. He really couldn't.

The next day he went round in his motor-car with the three small parcels. His Auntie Ellen was pleased to see him. She said he might come in and see Robert for just two minutes.

So in he went and gave him the three presents. Robert was simply delighted. He was in bed, and his bed was scattered with all kinds of presents.

"It's very kind of you, Derek," he said, undoing the parcels. "The top is lovely—and the book I'll read to-day—and the motor-car will just fit my new garage."

Derek was pleased. Then Robert said something surprising.

"I say, Derek," he said, "look! Someone has sent me a hooter—but I haven't got a car or a tricycle, so would you like it for *your* car? I know you've got that lovely red one and it hasn't got a hooter, has it?'

"Oh, Robert! Don't you really want it?" cried Derek, getting red with excitement, for the hooter was a much nicer one than he had meant to buy. "Oh, Robert, it's *exactly* what I wanted! Can you really spare it?"

"Of course I can," said Robert. "Mummy doesn't like the noise it makes, and I haven't got a car—so what's the use of it. Take it, and use it for your car!"

So Derek took it, and he fitted it to his car. And now, my goodness, you always know when he is

coming! Hoot-a-toot-too! Hoot-a-toot-too! goes that big hooter, and people think there's a *real* car coming and don't they jump out of the way!

Derek deserved it, don't you think so?

Somebody Saw!

IT WAS Sports Day at the big Boys' School. All the Johns, Bills, Peters and Mikes were hoping to win a prize of some kind.

How they practised their running and jumping and how they tried out the three-legged race for days beforehand! There were to be bicycle races too—quick ones and slow ones, and trick ones.

Most of the boys had bicycles, and they cleaned them up before the great day. George cleaned his up, too.

George's bicycle was very old. It wanted a coat of paint. Its pedals had very worn rubbers, and it was bent in several places.

"But it's a good old bike, all the same," George often said, when the other boys laughed at it. "I'm fond of it. It's taken me for miles and miles, and I've had jolly good times on it."

It *was* a good old bike, and George had never had a single accident on it. For one thing his Father made him read the Highway Code till he almost knew it by heart—and for another thing he made George learn his manners.

Not only manners at home and at school—but manners on the road! "You just remember that there are other people on the road, George," he said. "And don't forget that a spot of good manners can prevent an accident as often as keeping the Rules of the Road!"

So George waved on other bicyclists who wanted to pass him, instead of trying to out-race them, or swerving out at them as they passed. He stopped at the pedestrian crossings to let people walk over the road, instead of ringing his bell violently and making them jump. He put his hand out in good time before he turned a corner.

He was an excellent cyclist, and he had made up his mind to win one of the cycling prizes at the sports. If only he had a better bicycle!

"Harry's got one of the new racers," he thought as he cleaned his. "And John's just got a fine new one, as fast as any I've seen. And Fred's bike is a beauty."

He cycled off to school, in good time for the Sports. The parents had been asked to come too. They all turned up, hoping that their boys would win prizes. It was a hot, sunny day, just right for School Sports.

George was no good at running. He wasn't much good at jumping either, and Fred easily won the high jump. Harry won the long jump. Then came the three-legged race. George was tied to Jeffrey, who got a fit of giggles, and down they both went at once!

"Aren't you ever going to win something, George?" asked his Mother, when he went over to her. "We've

already had eight events, and you've been almost last in every one!"

"Wait till the cycling match," said George. "I'll win something there!"

But he didn't. He was a long way last in the speed race. How could anyone hope to go as fast as Harry on his new racer, or as Fred on his red and gold bike?

He didn't even win the slow bicycle race, because someone bumped into him and made him fall off. He was fourth in the trick-cycling, which was riding without touching the handle-bars as all.

"I would have been first if my bike hadn't been so old," he told his Mother. "You see, it's not properly balanced now. I haven't won a thing! I'm sorry, Mother, because though I don't mind, I know you're disappointed!"

"I am rather," said his Mother. "Your Father was so good at sports when he was a boy."

The Sports came to an end. The prizes were given out and George looked admiringly at Harry's new cricket-bat and the grand football that John went up to get. The prizes were really very good indeed.

Then the boys went home. "Now be careful, because you're all going off together," said the Head. "Don't act the goat—and remember, there are others on the road besides yourself!"

A lot of the boys did play the fool, of course. They always did. George couldn't help laughing when he saw Peter riding solemnly backwards down the road, instead of forwards, just as he had done in the trick cycling.

The boys didn't see a car following them slowly. They tore across the pedestrian crossing and made a woman with a pram scream, because she was already half-way across.

George stopped. "I say—don't be scared! Look, you've dropped your book." The woman was frightened and angry.

"You bad boys! Where are your manners, I'd like to know! I'll complain about you to your Head Master!"

George rode on. Behind came the car, very slowly. It stopped when George had got off his bicycle. George caught up the others, who were waiting for a traffic light to change. Two cars were there, too. The boys swerved their bicycles in front of the cars as soon as the lights changed, preventing them from getting off quickly. One of the motorists hooted

George waited, knowing that the cars would soon be well ahead of him. Then on he went again, and behind him came the car. He heard it and looked round. He swerved in to the kerb and waved it on courteously, and then waved on a man on a bicycle who seemed in a hurry.

The car stopped a little way in front. George saw two policemen in it. The driver beckoned to him Oh dear—had he done anything wrong?

"Name and address?" he said to poor George. "And school, please?"

George gave them, his heart sinking. "What have I done, sir?" he said.

"Done?" said the police-driver, with a broad smile. "Well, you've just won the Courtesy Prize for this town, that's all! We've been cruising round all day looking for someone on the roads who knows his Highway *Manners* as well as his Highway Rules—and you're the first person we've seen who knows them both."

"I *say*!" said George, astonished and delighted. "I've won a prize to-day, after all! I messed up everything I did at the Sports—and won a prize going home! What a bit of luck!"

The prize was a silver wrist-watch with his name on it—and it was presented by the police on the platform of George's school. The Head was delighted, and how the boys clapped George!

"Good old George! He's won something for the school! We've got the Courtesy Prize because of George."

George, still has the watch, it's a beauty. I know, because I've seen it!

The Tale of a Tail

JIMMY went to school just as you do. He did the same sums, and he did them quite well. He did the same reading, but he wasn't very good—and he did the same spelling, but he wasn't very good at that!

Now you may not think it matters whether you are a good speller or not—but just listen to what happened to Jimmy because he couldn't spell!

Jimmy loved being read to—but he always thought that stories were far too short. "I'd like one that is really, really long!" he complained to his mother. "Even the longest tale you read doesn't last long enough. Just as I am getting to know all the people in the story, it ends!"

"Well, perhaps you'll get one long enough for you some day!" said his mother. "There may be a brownie living in our garden. Why not write him a little note and ask him for a really long story to read?"

"That's a good idea!" said Jimmy. So he took a pencil and a piece of notepaper and wrote on it. This is what he said:

"Dear Brownie,

"I hope you live in my garden. Will you please

give me a long, long, long tail? Thank you. Love from

"Jimmy."

Now Jimmy spelt "tale" like this—"t-a-i-l," and what sort of a tail is that? Not one to read, certainly! But one to wear! And when the brownie found the note and read it he was puzzled. "Still," he said, "if the boy *wants* a long, long tail there must be some reason for it. So I'll give him one."

And do you know when Jimmy woke up next morning he found his legs all tangled up in a long, long tail, rather like a cat's, but brown like a cow's. At first Jimmy thought he had got mixed up with his pyjama string—but he soon found out what it was! He had grown a very long tail! He gave a scream and rushed into his mother's room, the tail dragging behind him like a brown snake.

"Mother! Mother! Look what's grown on me!" cried poor Jimmy. "I asked the brownie for a tale—and he's given me this instead!"

"Well, you must have spelt the word wrongly, Jimmy," said Mother. "You must have spelt 'tale' as 'tail'! So he's given you what you asked for! Oh dear, now whatever are we to do?"

Poor Jimmy! It wasn't much use trying to hide his tail because it was one with a very strong wag in it, and it insisted on wagging about all over the place. The children shouted with laughter, and his teacher was very cross, for she thought it was a tail that Jimmy had pinned on for a joke. When she heard what had happened she laughed.

"Didn't I tell you that spelling was important!" she said to Jimmy. "Now you'd better write another note to that brownie—and this time spell correctly!"

So Jimmy wrote another note, and this time he made no mistakes!

"Please take away my tail and give me a tale instead," he wrote to the brownie. The brownie was cross. "This boy is trying to be funny!" he said. "Well, I'll take away his tail—but I shan't give him a story!" So he snipped off Jimmy's tail—but he left nothing else instead!

Jimmy's top in spelling now. He doesn't want to make another mistake like that!

Never Mind!

HENRY had had a birthday. Mother had given him a train, Daddy had given him railway lines, and Auntie Nora had given him a book.

The postman had brought him three birthday cards and two birthday letters—and in each of the letters there was paper money!

In one letter there was a postal order for fifty pence from Uncle Fred. In the other there was a postal order for twenty five pence from Auntie Flo.

"I'm rich!" said Henry. "Mummy, can I spend this money, or must I save it?"

"What do Uncle Fred and Auntie Flo say in their letters?" asked Mummy. "You must do what they say."

"Well, Uncle Fred says, 'Please buy something you badly want with this money'; and Auntie Flo says, 'I am sending you twenty five pence to spend just how you like'," said Henry.

"Very well then," said Mummy. "You can spend your money, and not save it."

"Oh, good!" said Henry. "Well, I know what I shall buy with my fifty pence, Mummy! I shall buy a perfectly lovely paint-box that I saw in the window of the book-shop the other day. You know, I haven't got a paint-box, and I do want one very, very badly. Can I buy it to-day?"

"Yes," said Mummy. "And what are you going to buy with the other money?"

"The twenty five?" said Henry. "I don't know, Mummy. Sweets, perhaps. I'll just put it into my purse and see."

Henry set off to spend his fifty pence. He was so happy to think that he would have that beautiful paint-box. It was black, and inside there were twenty different colours, four tubes of paint, and four different-sized paint-brushes. It really was a wonderful box.

"I shall be able to paint marvellous pictures when I have that," thought Henry to himself. "Hallo, George! Hi! Look what I've got for my birthday!"

George came over to look. Henry took out the two bits of paper money from his purse, and showed them to George.

And then an awful thing happened. The wind swooped down and snatched one bit of paper right out of Henry's hand! It blew it away into the air, higher and higher. It blew it over the hedge—and then it was gone!

"Oh, quick! My fifty pence!" shouted Henry. "Quick! Get through the hedge and find it, George!"

George and Henry squeezed through the hedge and hunted for the paper money. But it had quite dis-

appeared. Billy the goat looked at them, and Henry stared at the goat.

"I feel sure Billy the goat's eaten my paper money," he said, almost in tears. "He's always eating all kinds of things, I saw him eating a newspaper yesterday—and he tries hard to eat tins and boxes too. Billy, have you eaten my fifty pence?"

The goat tossed his head and ran away. George was sorry for Henry.

"Never mind!" he said. "You've got your other paper money still, haven't you? You said you had two."

"Yes, I have," said George. "But this one is only for twenty five pence and won't buy me a paint-box like the one I wanted. I do feel unhappy."

"Never mind," said George again. "Buy some

chalks, Henry. You can make fine pictures with chalks, you know."

"All right," said Henry, feeling very miserable. He and George walked to the shop that sold books, papers, pencils, chalks and paints.

"That's a nice box of chalks," said George, pointing to one. "Get that, Henry. It's only twenty pence."

So Henry bought the box of chalks, and got five pence change from his postal order. "What shall I buy with the five pence?" he said.

"Look, there's a new *Sunny Stories* out," said George. "Buy that. It's only four pence, and there's a picture to chalk in it this week. And buy some sweets with the last penny."

So Henry went home with the box of chalks, a

Sunny Stories, and some sweets. He had given George two sweets and had promised to lend him the *Sunny Stories* when he had read it.

He told Mummy all about how he had lost his paper money, and she was very sorry. "Never mind," she said. "Never mind! You might have lost *both* your paper moneys, and that would have been worse. Never mind!"

"Well, I do mind," said poor Henry. "But I'm not going to make a fuss about it. Look, Mummy—do you see this competition in *Sunny Stories*? It's a picture we have to colour as nicely as ever we can. Do you think, if I do it very nicely, you would give me a stamp so that I could post the picture, and see if it is worth a prize?"

"Yes, certainly," said Mummy. "Do your very best."

"It's a pity I haven't got that lovely paint-box," sighed Henry. "If I had I could *paint* this picture instead of just chalking it."

He set to work on the picture. He did it beautifully. He didn't go over the line once, and as his chalks were all new and sharp, you can guess he made a really beautiful picture!

"That's splendid, Henry!" said Mummy. "You should certainly send it in. It might win a prize for you."

So Henry wrote his name and address under his picture, cut it out carefully, put it into an envelope, and sent it away to see if it was good enough for a prize.

And do you know, he found his name among the list of prize-winners when the results were printed! He could hardly believe his eyes! Just fancy! He had won a prize! When would it come? What would it be? Henry could hardly wait for the postman to come.

The prize came that very afternoon! The postman brought it in a brown-paper parcel, addressed to Henry Harrison. Henry took it and ran shouting to his mother.

"Mummy! Mummy! It's come! Will you undo it for me?"

Mummy cut the string. Henry undid the paper—and drew out his prize. What do you think it was? Guess! It was a big paint-box, full of the loveliest paints—just exactly what he wanted!

"Mummy!" he cried. "It's a much nicer one than the one I was going to buy! Just look at it! I've got a paint-box after all! Oh, I am *so* pleased—it's much, much nicer to win one than just to go and buy it!"

"Well, I *am* glad, Henry," said Mummy. "You didn't make a fuss about the paint-box you didn't get, and you do deserve this lovely one. Well done!"

And now Henry is busy going in for the next colouring competition—but *this* time he is using his new paint-box. He hopes you will win a prize one day too, and that it will be just exactly what you want!

The Wrong Bus

COLIN and Sue had gone to visit their Aunt Phyllis. She had given them a lovely time and then sent them off to catch their bus.

"You know which corner to wait at, don't you?" she said. "The one by the big oak tree at the end of the winding lane. It always stops there."

The children set off to catch the bus. Aunt Phyllis lived down in the country, and they loved the little winding lanes, the tall hedges, and the buttercup fields that lay all around.

"Is this the right lane we've turned down?" asked Sue suddenly. "I don't seem to remember that stile over there."

"Well, there's a big oak-tree, look, at the end of it," said Colin. "It must be all right. Let's stand here and wait."

There was a wooden seat at the end of the lane. On it several people were sitting. The children stared at them, rather surprised, for they looked a little peculiar.

There was an old man wearing a red hat with a long yellow feather in it. There were two old women, one with a brightly coloured parrot on her shoulder, and the other carrying a black cat with eyes as green as unripe apples. There was a young woman with a

baby. The baby was the prettiest little thing the children had ever seen. But it had rather queer ears that stuck out at each side of its little blue bonnet. They were pointed and rather long. The little thing was holding a rattle that rang a dear little tune.

The bus came along just then. The people got up to get in. It was a very gay-looking bus, with red wheels, blue sides and a yellow top.

Colin and Sue did not wait till the people who wanted to get out had stepped on to the road. They pushed their way on to the bus in front of everyone, elbowing the old man aside as they did so.

"What bad manners!" said the old man. But Colin and Sue didn't care. They had got on to the bus, and that was all that mattered to them.

They sat down. The bus was rather full. There was no room for one of the old women, and she stood in the gangway, holding on to a rail.

"Hey, boy! You get up and give this old woman your seat!" said the old man. "Don't you know your manners? Isn't your heart kind enough to pity an old dame who's been marketing and is tired out?"

"I shall pay for my seat, and I expect to sit in it," said Colin rudely. He always saw to it that he had the best of whatever was going. *He* wasn't going to get up and give anyone his seat, not he!

Someone got out just then and the old lady sank down into the seat with a sigh. Another woman got in, carrying a small child. She stood in the gangway. The old woman poked Sue in the back. "Get up and offer your seat!" she said. "You can't sit there and see somebody standing, carrying a heavy child."

"Why don't *you* get up?" said Sue cheekily.

"What terrible children!" said the old woman. Her black cat suddenly put out its paw and scratched Sue's hand. She gave a scream and hit the cat hard. It scratched her again at once.

"Even my cat thinks you're a bad child," said the old woman. "Sooty never scratches anyone unless they are horrid!"

The baby in front of Colin dropped its rattle. Colin saw it drop, but he didn't pick it up. He just sat there looking in front of him.

"Pick up my baby's rattle, please," said the young woman to Colin. "I can't very well bend down with baby on my knee."

Colin took no notice. *He* wasn't going to pick up a baby's rattle!

"What an unpleasant boy!" said the old man and picked up the rattle himself.

As he bent down something fell out of his pocket. He didn't notice it. But Colin did. It was a small leather purse! Colin put his foot on it at once, and then, pretending to drop his handkerchief, he bent down and picked up the purse. He was just putting it into his pocket when the old woman's parrot called out loudly:

"He's a thief, he's a thief, he's a thief!"

Everyone began to look at everyone else. Who was a thief? The old man saw Colin's face turning red. He put his hand into his pocket and found that his purse was gone!

"Have you got my purse?" he cried. "Yes, you have, you bad boy! You must have picked it up. Give it to me back at once."

Colin looked sulkily. "I haven't got your purse," he said.

"He's telling stories, he's telling stories," said the annoying parrot and squawked loudly.

The conductor came up. He slipped his hand into Colin's pocket and took out the pursc. Everyone gasped in horror.

"These children are not only bad-mannered, they are dishonest and untruthful and unkind," said the old man, shocked.

"Their mother and father must be simply *terrible*!" said the old woman with the cat.

"Yes. They must have taught their children all the wrong things," said the old man, shaking his head. "Very, very sad. They look quite nice children—but they're not, they're not!"

"I think we had better take them to the Wise Woman," said the old woman with the parrot. "She might be able to take away their bad father and mother and give them new ones who would teach them kindness and good manners and honesty. Parents are no use unless they do that."

"My mother is very good and sweet!" cried Sue. "Don't you dare to say anything against her!"

"And my father's a very busy doctor, who helps a lot of people, so don't you dare to say he's bad!" shouted Colin, feeling suddenly afraid. These people in the bus were queer. Had he and Sue taken the wrong bus?

"We can't believe you," said the old man. "If you had good parents, who taught you the right things, you would behave well, you would have good manners, you would be kind. But you are really horrid children."

"And we have always noticed that horrid children usually have horrid parents," said the old woman with the parrot. The parrot nodded its head violently.

"How could you be a thief if your parents were honest?" said the old man. "You must have copied them! How could you be untruthful if they were truthful? Children always copy their father and mother. We know exactly what the fathers and mothers are like when we see their children."

"I tell you my father is kind and honest and everyone loves him!" said Colin, scared.

"And my mother has the best manners of anyone I know!" wept Sue. "She has, she has!"

"Can't believe it!" said the old man. "It's quite impossible. Your mother must be just like you. I expect she would push her way on to a bus out of her turn, and get a seat before anyone else, and let old men and women stand, and she would steal someone's purse, and——"

"Oh, oh, how unkind you are to say such things!" sobbed Sue, thinking of her kind, gentle mother. "Mummy isn't like that, she isn't! She's always kind."

"We'd better go to the Wise Woman and look up the names of these children's parents and see if by any chance what they say is true," said the old man. "Conductor, will you stop the bus at the Wise Woman's cottage, please?"

Half a minute later the bell rang and the bus

stopped. Out got everyone, even the cat. They made their way to a queer little tumbledown cottage nearby, pushing the two scared children in front of them.

"We took the wrong bus!" whispered Colin to Sue. "Goodness knows who these people are, or where we've come to!"

The Wise Woman was a wonderful person. She was old, but she had a very young face. She was dressed in a long robe of purest blue, like the summer sky outside. There was something queer about this dress, for it shifted and shone like mist.

The old man explained what they had come for. The Wise Woman turned her eyes on to the two children. "I see badness and unkindness in them," she said in a voice that sounded like the murmuring of waves. "Their hearts are hard. Yes, I think we

must change their parents and give them better ones. No child can grow up right if it has bad parents, who spoil it or make it unkind and untrustworthy."

She took up a long silver staff and began to point it first at Sue and then at Colin. "What are you doing?" cried Colin in alarm. "We don't want new parents. We love ours. They are good and kind!"

"Perhaps I had better make sure that these children's parents *are* bad," said the Wise Woman, and she took up a round mirror. She looked deeply into it. Colin tried to peep into it, too, but, instead of his own face, all he could see was a swirling mist.

The Wise Woman was silent for a few minutes. Everyone waited patiently. Sue began to tremble. How dreadful if their bad behaviour lost them their father and mother. She didn't want new ones.

"Now this is a strange thing," said the Wise Woman, putting down the mirror. "These children have told the truth about their father and mother. They are kind, good parents, but they are too gentle and too trustful. They believe that their children are honest and sweet and kind—and because the children are deceitful, and only behave badly when they are away from home, their parents have no idea what bad manners and hard hearts they really have!"

"Bad children come from bad parents," said the old man obstinately. "We've always known that. Look at a child, watch the way he behaves—and you know what kind of a mother he's got!"

"That's right," said the old woman with the parrot. "When I see a child with no manners, I say:

'His mother doesn't know any either, so he hasn't been taught!' Wise Woman, change these children's parents. They must be bad, whatever your mirror says."

Sue began to sob loudly. Colin went very pale. "Please," he said, "give us another chance. I know that a bad father and mother do make bad children —but this time it's we who are in the wrong. We wouldn't learn. We've got good parents, really we

have—but we've let them down. We behave as if we've got bad ones."

"But we won't again," said Sue, wiping her eyes. "We never thought that people judged our parents by the way *we* behaved. If I'd known you were thinking that our father and mother were so bad, I'd have behaved better. But I will now, if you'll give us a chance."

"I always give people chances," said the Wise Woman, looking at the children with her deep, clear eyes. "You, too, shall have your chance. Catch the next bus home—the right one this time. You caught the wrong bus before—but if you've learnt a lesson from me and all these people, it will not matter. Now go!"

The children fled away at once. They saw a bus rumbling down the street. It stopped nearby and they jumped on it. They looked round. Yes—the people looked quite ordinary this time. There were no black cats, no talkative parrots, no babies with pointed ears.

At the next stop an old lady got in. At once Colin stood up and offered her his seat. She sat down gratefully.

"What a nice-mannered child!" she said to her neighbour. "He's got a good mother, no doubt about that!"

What a strange adventure, wasn't it? I wonder what people think *your* father and mother are like when they watch how you behave? Think for a minute and you'll know!

Untidy William

THERE was once a boy who was very untidy. His name was William, and his mother was always scolding him for being so untidy.

"You never put *any*thing away, William!" she would say. "You leave your shoes out—you leave your cap on the floor—you throw your coat down. It's simply dreadful."

"Sorry, Mother!" said William cheerfully.

"You're *not* sorry!" said his mother. "If you were, you would try to do better. I am always clearing up after you—and yet you never try to help me."

"Well, I *will* try!" said William. So the next day he really tried. He hung up his cap on the peg, and he put his shoes into the cupboard. Gracious, he did feel good! But as he dropped his coat on the floor and left his scarf on the stairs, he didn't really do very well after all!

He went upstairs. He opened the desk he had there, to find a favourite pencil. He couldn't find it, so he scrabbled about in the desk just as if he were a dog scratching in the ground for a hidden bone—and, of course, everything went flying out of his desk on to the floor!

Did William pick them up? Of course not! Hadn't he hung up his cap on the peg and put his shoes

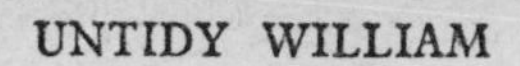

away in the cupboard? Well, that was tidiness enough for one day, as far as William was concerned.

Then William sat down on the clean bed-cover and creased that. He knocked his pyjamas on to the floor and didn't pick them up. His mother came in to speak to him and saw the untidy mess in his bedroom.

"William! I thought you were going to try and be really tidy to-day!" she said. "And you seem to be worse than ever!"

"Well, Mother, I like that!" said William. "Didn't you see how I had hung up my cap on its peg, and put my shoes away in the cupboard? You might have noticed that, I do think!"

"All I noticed was that your coat was on the floor in the hall, and I tripped over your scarf as I came upstairs!" said his Mother. "William, I don't know what to do with you."

She went out of the room. William sat and thought for a minute. Then he got up.

"I've often read in stories that people can get spells from the fairy-folk to put things right when they are untidy or untruthful or greedy," he thought. "I've a good mind to go to old Dame Goody and ask her if she knows of one to keep me tidy. Then I wouldn't keep getting into trouble with Mother. It would be so nice to be tidy without having to keep on remembering it."

He put on his outdoor things and went up the hill to where old Dame Goody lived. She was a funny little old lady, and she had most peculiar eyes. Sometimes they looked grey and sometimes they looked green. That was because her grandmother had been first cousin to a fairy.

Well, Dame Goody was surprised to see William, for usually the children were rather afraid of her, though she was a kind old dame who wouldn't have hurt anybody for anything.

"Good morning, Dame Goody," said William. "I expect you know that I'm awfully untidy, don't you?"

"Well, I can see it," said the old woman, looking down at William's shoes, which were both undone, and at his coat, which had the buttons done up wrongly.

"Do you think you could possibly give me a spell to make me tidy without my bothering much about it?" asked William. "I would so much like one. I could pay you for it. I've got five pence in my money-box."

"Well, I believe I *have* got an old, old spell tucked away somewhere that my grandmother had by her," said Dame Goody, her eyes suddenly looking very green. "And if it would do for a tidy-spell, you can have it for five pence."

She went off into the back-room, and William heard her hunting in drawers for the old, old spell. At last she came back, smiling. She held a funny little tin in her hand. It was bright blue, and at the top it had a head instead of a lid.

"I've found the spell," said Dame Goody. "I'll scatter it over you, and you will then find that your things will all be terribly tidy!"

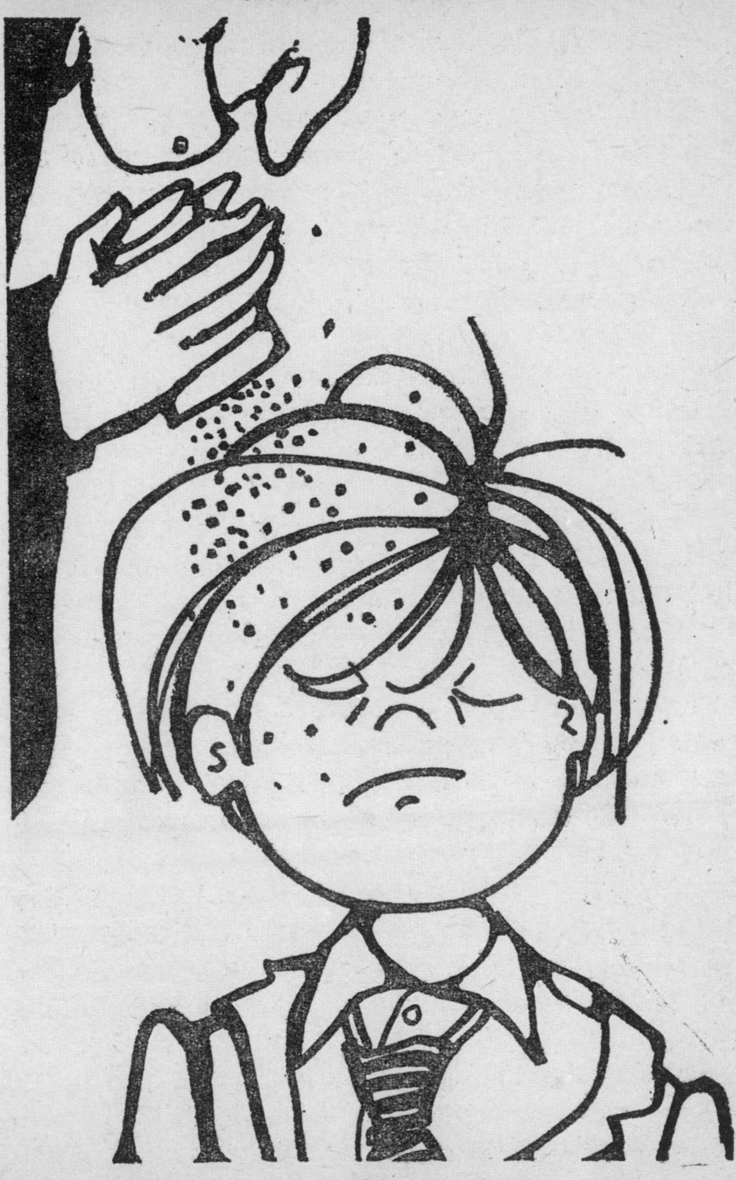

"But *I* want to be tidy," said William, "not my things."

"Well, it's easier to make your things tidy than you," said Dame Goody. "Now stand still, please!"

William stood still. Dame Goody took off the funny little wooden head that was on the top of the tin instead of a lid, and scattered a blue powder all over William.

"I feel as if you are peppering me!" said William, beginning to sneeze. "A-tish-oo!"

Dame Goody muttered a string of magic words that sounded very queer to William. Then she clapped the lid on to the tin, and nodded her head at him.

"The spell will work tomorrow morning," she said. "I hope it's all right. It's rather old, you see. It may have gone a bit wrong."

"What should it do?" asked William.

"Well, it should make anything belonging to you put itself neatly away," said Dame Goody. "Your pencils should put themselves away in the box. Your cap should hang itself up on the peg. Your clothes should fold themselves up neatly when you take them off, and put themselves on a chair or away in a drawer."

"That sounds marvellous!" said William, pleased. "Thank you, Dame Goody. I shall now be known as the tidiest boy in the kingdom!" He went off, smiling, wishing that the next day would come quickly.

It came. William awoke, dressed himself, and then threw down his pyjamas on the floor on purpose to see if the spell was working.

And do you know, those pyjamas solemnly got up, folded themselves neatly, and put themselves into the pyjama-case on the bed. It was most extraordinary to watch them.

"This is fine!" thought William. "Simply fine!"

He threw his tooth-brush on to the floor. It at once flew up into the air, and settled itself calmly into the tooth-mug. William was very pleased indeed.

He went downstairs, in good time for breakfast. His father was there, reading the newspaper, and he looked up as William came in. "Hallo, son," he said, and then buried himself behind the paper again. "Sit down and get on with your porridge," his mother called from the kitchen. "I'm just getting the bacon and eggs!"

William sat down. He was just about to put sugar on his porridge, when something most peculiar happened. His shoes came off, and his stockings unpeeled from his legs!

William looked down in astonishment. Whatever could be happening? To his enormous surprise he saw his shoes hopping neatly together over the floor. They went out of the door, and he heard them going to the hall-cupboard! Well, well, well!

His stockings rolled themselves into a neat ball, and then bowled themselves out of the door too. They went upstairs and put themselves into a drawer.

Then William's coat took itself off William and flew away to hang itself up. His shirt and tie came off and his shorts. They all folded themselves up very

neatly indeed and then went upstairs to put themselves away.

And there was William sitting at the breakfast-table in his vest! He simply didn't know what to do.

"My goodness! The spell *has* gone wrong!" he thought in dismay. "Instead of waiting until I was untidy, my things have put themselves away now! I'd better creep upstairs before anyone sees me and dress again."

Well, William was just about to creep away when his mother came into the room with the bacon and eggs. She saw William sitting at the table in his vest and she almost dropped the dish in amazement.

"*William!* Why haven't you dressed? Don't you know that you are only in your vest? Really, is this the way to come down to breakfast? What in the world are you thinking of?"

Daddy looked up in surprise. How he stared when he saw poor William in nothing but his vest!

"Is this a joke?" he asked. "Because, if so, I don't think it is at all amusing! Boys who come down in their vests ought to be punished."

William fled upstairs. Goodness, this was dreadful! He didn't like it at all!

William found his things in the drawers and in his cupboard and dressed himself again. He tied his shoe-laces firmly in a knot, in case his shoes thought of hopping off again. He did up all his coat-buttons tightly.

"It would be simply dreadful if they all came off again," he thought. "I really don't know what Daddy would say!"

Well, nothing happened at breakfast-time except that a spoon which William dropped, hopped up to the table again on its own, and put itself neatly by William's plate.

"Now that's good," thought William. "That's the sort of thing that I wanted the spell for. If only it goes on working like that, it will be fine."

But it didn't! William put on his cap, coat, scarf, and gloves, and went to catch the bus to go to school. And in the bus, his cap, coat, scarf, and gloves all undid themselves, and sailed away out of the bus door! They fled home, hung themselves up, or put themselves in a drawer—and there was poor cold William shivering in the bus without any of his outdoor clothes! There was only an old man in the bus besides William. The conductor was on the top

of the bus. The old man was rather astonished to see William without any cap or coat, but he said nothing.

But Mr. Brown, his teacher, said quite a lot. "William! How is it that you have come to school like this? Really, what are you thinking of to come without your cap or coat? You will catch a dreadful cold on this bitter winter day!"

William couldn't say that his things had flown away by themselves, so he said nothing. He went into his classroom and sat down.

And immediately all the pencils, rubber, and pocket-knife in his pocket hopped out to the desk and put themselves tidily into his box! Mr. Brown heard the noise and looked up.

"Is it really necessary to make all that noise with your pencil-box, William?" he asked. William said he was sorry, and glared at his pencils and rubber and knife. His pencil-box lid shut down with a snap.

And then the books on William's desk decided that the right place for them was the book-case! So they took a jump and landed on the book-shelf with a crash. Everyone looked up.

"William! Did *you* throw your books on to the shelf?" asked Mr. Brown. "What *can* be the matter with you to-day?"

"I didn't throw them," said William.

"Well, I suppose you will tell me that they jumped there themselves!" said Mr. Brown.

"That's just what they did do," said poor William.

"Any more of this behaviour and you will stay in at the end of the morning," said Mr. Brown sternly.

William looked worried. He did hope that the spell wouldn't work any more that morning! Oh, why had he ever tried to get a tidy-spell? It was getting him into great difficulties.

After playtime that morning, the boys settled down to a history lesson. Mr. Brown was teaching them about the people of long ago. William listened well, for he loved history stories.

And then he felt his right shoe twisting about on his foot! The spell was beginning to work again. The shoe wanted to take itself home and put itself away into the cupboard. But William had tied the laces very tightly and it couldn't get itself off!

William tried to keep his foot still—but the spell worked very hard, and the shoe twisted about so much that it twisted William's foot with it.

"William! Is it *you* fidgeting?" cried Mr. Brown at last. "Keep your feet still!"

But that was just what William couldn't do! The spell began to work in both shoes, and so both William's feet began to fidget about. Mr. Brown was very cross.

"Stand up, William," he said. "If you can't *sit* still, perhaps you can stand still!"

So William had to stand for the rest of the history lesson, and he didn't like it at all. His shoes twisted about for a while, then grew tired and stopped.

At the end of the morning came a lesson that William liked very much. It was carpentering. William was making a ship. He had a hammer, screw-driver, chisel, pincers, gimlet, and nails of his own. He went with the other boys to get his tools from the woodwork cupboard.

Well, the spell began to work again as soon as

William was happily hammering nails into his ship. He put down his tools for a moment and took up his ship to ask Mr. Brown if it was all right. And when he came back to his desk, his tools had disappeared!

"Who's taken my tools?" asked William, looking all round. Nobody had! It was very mysterious. Then William wondered if the spell was working again. Perhaps his tools had put themselves away in the box in the woodwork cupboard. So he went to look—and sure enough, there they were! William took them out, whilst all the boys looked on in astonishment.

"Why did you put them away in the middle of the lesson?" asked Dick.

William didn't answer. He didn't know what to say. He set to work again.

Then he went to look at a submarine that another boy was making, and when he got back to his own work—gracious goodness, his tools had disappeared *again*!

William knew where they were, of course—in the tool-box! So he went to get them again. Mr. Brown looked up.

"William! Are you going to spend *all* the lesson in going to the cupboard and back for tools?" he asked.

Poor William! All he could say was, "Sorry, Mr. Brown!" He was quite glad when the lesson came to an end.

Just as the boys were lined up to be dismissed at half-past twelve, William felt his coat coming undone. Goodness, were his clothes going to rush off again? No, no—he really couldn't bear it! William clutched his coat to himself very tightly, and held it there.

"William! Have you got a pain or something?" asked Mr. Brown in surprise. "Really, you are behaving in a very queer manner to-day!"

William was glad to get outside—and only just in time too! His coat tore itself off him and flew down the road like a mad thing. Then his shoes and stockings and garters flew off too. William simply couldn't stop them. He stared in the greatest dismay.

The boys shouted with laughter. "Look! The wind has blown away William's clothes! Oh, how funny!"

Poor old William! By the time he got home he had only his shorts and his vest left, and he was very cold indeed. He crept in at the back door, hoping that his mother wouldn't notice him. He slipped upstairs. There, neatly hanging up, was his coat. Folded tidily in the drawer was his shirt. His stockings were rolled up in their drawer, with the garters beside them. His shoes were side by side by the bed.

"I simply can't stand this!" thought William, in despair. "I'm going to go to old Dame Goody at once and beg her to do something about this dreadful spell."

So he dressed himself again quickly and slipped out of the back-door to go to old Dame Goody's. He banged loudly on her door and she opened it in surprise.

"Dame Goody! That spell worked all wrong!" said William. "It's done the most dreadful things. Please do something about it."

"Dear me, I'm sorry," said Dame Goody. "Well,

step inside a moment. I've got a special drink that stops spells from working if they are no longer needed. Now, where did I put it?"

She took what looked like a large-size medicine bottle from a cupboard and poured out a drink for William. Gracious, it did taste horrid!

"Now, the spell won't work any more as long as you try to be tidy yourself," said Dame Goody. "It will only work if you are very untidy again. So I should be careful if I were you, William!"

"Goodness! I shall be the tidiest boy in the world!" said William, and he ran off home.

Well, he *isn't* the tidiest boy in the world, but he's a lot better. I watch him whenever I see him just in case I might suddenly see his tie whisk itself away or his cap fly off home to its peg. It really would be fun to see that, wouldn't it!

Sammy the Scribbler

THERE was once a little boy called Sammy. The other children called him Sammy the Scribbler because he scribbled over everything.

He chalked on walls. He scribbled in pencil over desks and tables. He ran a white chalk across every fence he came to. He was really a perfect nuisance.

"My mother won't let me scribble or chalk over walls and fences," said Tom. "She says it's an ugly thing to do."

"Mine doesn't mind," said Sammy. "She never scolds me for that. I was out with her yesterday, and I wrote my name all over the fence of my auntie's house. My mother didn't tell me not to."

"Then she must be the sort of mother who spoils her children," said Hilda. "I guess your auntie won't be pleased when she sees the mess you have made of her fence."

Hilda was quite right when she said Sammy's mother spoilt him. She hated to say "No" to him, and she hated to scold him. So he was allowed to do all sorts of things that the other children were for-

bidden to do. And that was very bad for Sammy, as you can guess.

Well, he went on scribbling. He scribbled on the wall of the village hall. He put red and white crosses all over the new fence round the school playground. He scribbled over the wall of the new cloakroom in his school. He scribbled silly things there and made the teacher very angry.

He scribbled "Hilda is silly" and "Tom is a baby" and "Will is greedy". Then, when the teacher wanted to know who had done the scribbling, Sammy wouldn't own up.

The other children didn't give him away, for they were not tell-tales, and the whole class was punished by being kept in at playtime.

They were very angry indeed. Afterwards Tom went to Sammy and said: "Now you take a wet cloth and go and wash out every single thing you have scribbled in our new cloakroom. You ought to be ashamed of yourself."

Sammy had to wash out his scribblings, but he wasn't ashamed of himself. He soon began again!

One day he went out into the country for a walk. He went into a wood and down a little narrow path that looked like a rabbit path. And very soon he came to a very clean and tidy little cottage.

Its walls had just been whitewashed. They were smooth and white and clean. Sammy looked at them and his fingers went into his pockets to get out his coloured chalks. Oh, how fine it would be to write all kinds of things on that nice white wall! He could draw pictures, too. He would draw his teacher.

He went cautiously round the cottage to see if anyone was in. But it was empty. Nobody came to see who was knocking at the door. Sammy meant to ask for a cup of water if anyone did come. "Good," said Sammy. "There's no one here. I can have a fine time scribbling!"

So he began. He scribbled his name heaps of times. He drew his teacher. He drew the other children and put something rude under each one.

He drew Tom and scribbled underneath, "This is Tom. He is a mean boy." Then he drew Hilda, and wrote underneath, "This is Hilda. She tells stories instead of the truth." He drew Will and wrote, "What a horrid boy Will is! He always has dirty knees."

He had a perfectly lovely time. He finished by writing his name "Sammy Brown, Sammy Brown" in every empty space that was left.

Then he went home, pleased with himself. He had never had such a lovely big scribble in his life before!

Now that night, when he was in bed, a knock came at his window. Sammy was startled. People don't usually knock at windows. They knock at doors.

The knock came again, more loudly.

"Come in!" said Sammy. And somebody opened the window and came in!

It was a brownie, a small man with a long beard, dressed in green. He had very bushy eyebrows that almost hid his eyes and made it seem as if he was frowning hard.

He looked at Sammy and spoke in a stern voice, "Is your name Sammy Brown?"

"Yes," said Sammy. "Who are you?"

"I'm the brownie who lives in the whitewashed cottage," said the brownie, and he glared at Sammy. Sammy began to feel uncomfortable.

"Oh, are you?" he said. "I don't think I know it."

"Oh yes you do," said the brownie. "You scribbled disgusting things all over my nice clean walls. Horrid little nuisance of a boy! How dare you?"

"How—how did you know it was me?" stammered Sammy, frightened.

"Well, you signed your name all over the wall, didn't you?" said the brownie, coming close to the bed. Sammy saw that he had green eyes, a sign that he belonged to the fairy folk. "Yes, it was there all right. 'Sammy Brown, Sammy Brown, Sammy Brown.' So I found out where Sammy Brown lived and came to see you about it."

"Well, I haven't done anything very dreadful," said Sammy.

"It's a disgusting, ill-mannered, mean habit," said the brownie. "Didn't you write horrid things about your friends? Yes, you did! Mean little boy. You deserve to be taken out of bed, turned over, and spanked!"

"Now, look here, I shall call my mother if you do anything like that," said Sammy in alarm. "My mother doesn't mind my scribbling, neither does my father. So I don't know why *you* should mind. Go away."

It wasn't true that his father didn't mind. His father did mind. He was always cross if he found Sammy's scribbles anywhere. But his mother spoilt him, as you have heard.

"Dear me!" said the brownie, raising his enormous eyebrows. "So you have a mother and father as bad as yourself! Well, well. I'd better punish them as well."

He didn't say a word more. He went out of the room and shut the door. Sammy did not dare to follow in case the brownie really did spank him. He went to sleep. In the morning he woke up to hear his father being very angry!

"Who's done this? How dare Sammy do this? Sammy, come here!"

Sammy was frightened. What had happened? His father sounded dreadfully cross. He crept out of bed and went to the bathroom, where his father was.

All round the nice yellow walls were scribblings—and scribblings just like Sammy's! There were silly drawings, too. One was of his father, and underneath was written in writing very like Sammy's "This is Daddy. He makes silly jokes".

Sammy shook and shivered. His father glared at him, very angry. "How many times have I told you not to do this kind of thing? How dare you do it in the bathroom? I shall spank you hard."

Sammy's mother came in, frightened. "Oh, no, don't spank poor Sammy," she said. "He didn't mean to be naughty, did you, Sammy? He's only little, Daddy." But Mother changed her mind when she went downstairs and saw that there were scribblings in chalk all over the dining-room wall too! And there was a picture of her, too, with writing underneath. "This is Mother. She lets me do as I like."

"Oh, you bad boy!" she said, and she gave Sammy the hardest slap he had ever had. "Daddy, you're right. He badly needs a spanking."

"He's going to get it," said Daddy. "What have you to say about this, Sammy?"

"Only that I didn't do it, I didn't, I didn't, I didn't!" said poor Sammy. "Do believe me."

But Daddy didn't. "Then who did do it, if you didn't?" he asked scornfully.

"It was the brownie who came in at my window last night," said Sammy, beginning to cry. "He said he would punish me, and punish you and Mother, too. He said you were as bad as I was."

"Well, well, well," said his father. "Perhaps we *are* as bad as you are, because we haven't stopped you doing these silly things. But I'm afraid I don't believe that a brownie came in at your window in the night, Sammy. That isn't true."

"But it *is* true!" wept Sammy. "I chalked on the walls of his cottage in the wood, and he came to see me about it. It was the brownie who scribbled, I know it was."

But not even Mother believed that. She was very angry indeed. Sammy got a hard spanking and went to bed for the whole of the day. The next day he had to wash off all the brownie's scribblings, and it took him all the morning. "I've a good mind to go and scribble on the brownie's cottage, and say, 'The brownie is a mean fellow' " thought Sammy. But he didn't. He never did any scribbling on walls or fences again.

"That's the end of our spoiling Sammy," said his father. And it was. His father and mother were strict with him after that, scolded him when he needed it, and saw that he did what he ought to do.

And Sammy is so much nicer now! You'd never know he was once horrid little spoilt Sammy the Scribbler. He went one day to the wood to find the white cottage again, for he wanted to say he was sorry to the brownie for having spoilt his walls. But there was no cottage there, and no brownie either.

I expect he moved himself and his house to a place where Sammy could never come to scribble, don't you?

Tiresome Tilda

ONCE upon a time there was a little girl called Matilda, but everyone called her Tilda for short. She lived with her Mother and Father in a nice little house, and she had just as many toys as you have.

But Tilda was very tiresome. She hated putting on her coat to go out of doors on a cold day. She grumbled about putting on goloshes on a rainy day. She wouldn't wash her hands before meals, and she didn't seem to know what a hairbrush was for!

"You're always fussing me, Mummy!" she said to her Mother. "Why can't I do as I like?"

"Don't be rude, Tilda," said her Mother. "Nobody in this world can do as they like, and everyone would hate them if they *did*! It's only because I love you that I want you to be warm and clean and grow up healthy and lovable."

"Well, I wish you didn't love me so much, then," said Tilda rudely. "I think it's a nuisance! I wish I lived with someone who didn't love me so much and wasn't so fussy!"

"Tilda!" said her Mother, very grieved. Wasn't she a rude little girl?

Tilda went off to school. When she came home again her Mother was not at the door to welcome her. There was no one there, so Tilda marched round to the back-door and looked in.

Her mother wasn't in the kitchen either. But Tilda's Aunt Fanny was there, cooking the dinner.

Tilda stared in surprise.

"Good morning, Tilda," said Aunt Fanny briskly. "I expect you are wondering where Mummy is. Well, I came this morning and found her looking ill and unhappy. She told me that you had said you wished you didn't live with someone who loved you so much —so I've sent her for a little holiday, and I've come to look after you instead!"

"Oh," said Tilda. She didn't like Aunt Fanny. She knew that Aunt Fanny didn't like *her*, either! Aunt Fanny said Tilda was a tiresome, disobedient girl!

"You've got what you want, you see," said Aunt Fanny, taking the meat out of the oven. "I don't love you, so I shan't fuss over you. You can do what you like. I shan't care a bit. So perhaps you will be happy. Dinner will be ready in five minutes."

Tilda went out into the garden. She didn't like the idea of Aunt Fanny looking after her at all. But perhaps it would be rather fun to have somebody who wouldn't fuss about things. Anyway, Tilda wouldn't wash her hands or brush her hair for dinner! She would play on her swing instead.

So Tilda played on her swing, waiting for Aunt Fanny to call her to dinner. Mummy always had to call Tilda two or three times before she came.

But Aunt Fanny didn't call Tilda!

Tilda waited till she was really hungry, and then she went indoors, ready to grumble because dinner was so long in coming. But to her surprise, Aunt Fanny was just finishing her *pudding*!

"Oh, you didn't tell me dinner was ready!" said Tilda.

"I told you it would be ready in five minutes' time," said Aunt Fanny. "You didn't come, so I thought you didn't want any. I've put the meat away. There's a bit of pudding left if you like."

Tilda was angry. She sat down and ate the pudding, but she was still hungry when she had finished. Aunt Fanny cleared away. Tilda went out into the garden again.

She had a hole in her stocking. Her hands were dirty. Her hair was in a tangle. "Anyway, Aunt Fanny won't fuss about those things!" thought Tilda. "I'll do them in a hurry just before I pop off to school again. And I certainly shan't bother to change my stockings!"

She took a book and began to read. She forgot all about school-time, and Aunt Fanny didn't bother to remind her. It made Tilda jump when she heard the school bell. "Oh, Aunt Fanny, you might have reminded me of the time," she cried. "Mummy always does."

"Oh, Mummy fusses you, as you said!" said Aunt Fanny. "I'm never one to fuss. If you want to be late, *be* late!"

There was no time even to wash. Tilda sped down

the road and got to school just after the door had been shut. Miss Brown, the teacher, opened the door.

"Tilda, you are late," she said crossly. "We were just getting ready to go for a nature-walk as it is such a beautiful afternoon. But, good gracious, Tilda—do you suppose I'm going to take you looking like that! Look at your hands! And your untidy hair! And for the first time I see you have a hole in your stocking! I think your Mother must be away."

"Yes, Miss Brown, she is," said Tilda in a small voice.

"And you can't even be trusted to wash your own hands!" said Miss Brown. "I'm ashamed of you. You will stay here this afternoon and I shall take the others."

So Tilda had to stay behind and do writing and sums. She was very upset, and she cried. What a pity Mummy had gone away! She would never have let Tilda go to school looking like that.

When Tilda got home again, Aunt Fanny was baking cakes. Tilda was delighted. She was *very* hungry, for she hadn't had much dinner, and she sniffed the good smell happily.

"Oh, Aunt Fanny! How nice of you to bake cakes for me!" she said.

"Good gracious, child, they're not for you!" said Aunt Fanny. "You can have one or two if you like—but I'm baking them for Mrs. White, who is coming to tea with me. I don't want you to have tea with us, you look such a sight—you can have tea by yourself here in the kitchen, and I shall have Mrs. White in the drawing-room."

Tilda felt hurt. Mummy always let her have tea with visitors, and dressed her up nicely—though Tilda did grumble at that!

"There are your buns," said Aunt Fanny, and put two on a plate.

"Oh!" said Tilda. "They are ginger buns! I hate ginger, Aunt Fanny. You know I do! You might have made some chocolate ones. I love those."

"My dear Tilda, I don't fuss over you as your kind Mother does!" said Aunt Fanny. "She loves you, and I don't. I might love you if you were a bit nicer to your Mother—but who could love a child who is always grumbling and whining. *I* like ginger buns, and so does Mrs. White. I didn't bother about *you*!"

Tilda said no more. She sat down to her tea. There was brown bread and butter and plum jam. Tilda was so hungry that she ate six slices, though if her Mother had been at home she would have grumbled to her because there was only plum jam instead of strawberry or raspberry!

Tilda went out to play after tea. She played horses by herself and galloped down the path. She knocked her foot against the grass edge and fell over on to her knees.

She grazed one knee and made it bleed. Tilda began to howl. Mummy always came rushing out when Tilda howled, and made such a fuss of her, and bound up the knee, and kissed Tilda. But Aunt Fanny didn't.

Aunt Fanny came to the window and called crossly. "Tilda! Stop that dreadful noise! Do you want to be sent to bed?"

"Aunt Fanny, I've hurt my knee, and I want it bathed and bandaged!" wailed Tilda.

"What a fuss about nothing!" said Aunt Fanny. "Go and bathe it yourself, and put a clean hanky round. I'm not coming to fuss over you! I thought that was just the sort of thing you hated!"

So Tilda had to bathe her own knee, and she felt very hurt and unhappy. She went to show Aunt Fanny how neatly she had bandaged it, but Aunt Fanny sent her off at once.

"You are too untidy and dirty to see a visitor," she said.

"But can I come in if I go and wash and tidy myself?" begged Tilda.

"Certainly!" said Aunt Fanny. So Tilda went and washed herself and did her hair and put on a clean dress. But when she went downstairs again. Mrs. White had gone. It was most disappointing.

"It's bedtime now," said Aunt Fanny.

"But I don't go till seven o'clock!" said Tilda. "It's only half-past six. And Mummy always reads to me first."

"Well, I want you out of the way," said Aunt Fanny. "I don't like having you around, as your Mother does. And as for reading to you, I couldn't be bothered. That's what I call making a fuss of you—and your Mother told me that you hate fussing. Go along now, hurry up to bed."

So Tilda had to go. She was very sad. She did her teeth carefully, had a bath and wished Mummy were there to wash her, and plait her hair. Then she got into bed.

She waited for Aunt Fanny to come and say good-night. But she didn't come. Tilda began to cry.

"What's the matter?" said Aunt Fanny, putting her head in at the door.

"Aren't you going to kiss me and tuck me up?" said poor Tilda. "I do wish Mummy were here. She always sees that my teeth are cleaned, and washes my back for me, and brushes my hair. She never dreams of not kissing me and tucking me up. I wish she'd come back. I don't like not being fussed. I want Mummy to love me and fuss me again."

"So you made a mistake, Tilda?" said Aunt Fanny. "You were wrong—you do really like someone who

loves you and fusses you and comforts you?"

"Yes, I do," said Tilda. "And when Mummy comes back I'm going to fuss over *her* a bit! I shall love her a lot, and I shan't ever let her go away again!"

And, then, what do you think? Mummy came into the room and took Tilda into her arms and hugged her. She had just come back and had heard what Tilda had said. Aunt Fanny slipped off home, and left Mummy with Tilda. Wasn't Tilda happy!

"I can't do without you, Mummy!" she said. "You just fuss me and tell me to do things all you like—I won't mind a bit so long as you're there to love me. And I'm going to love you ten times more, so look out!"

What a trick Aunt Fanny played on Tilda, didn't she! I wouldn't like it played on me!

He Wouldn't Brush His Hair

"GORDON, you haven't brushed your hair again!" said Mother.

"Oh, Mother—you always fuss so about my hair!" grumbled Gordon. "It's always: 'You haven't washed your hands—you haven't brushed your hair—you haven't wiped your feet!' "

"That will do, Gordon," said Daddy. "Go and brush your hair at once. And if you forget again, after Mother has told you, I shall not give you your Saturday five pence."

Gordon went off sulkily and brushed his hair. He had the kind of hair that really does need to be well brushed. It stuck out all over the place, and had to be brushed and brushed before it looked neat and tidy.

"Horrible hair! Tiresome hair!" said Gordon, and he flattened it down with his brush. Then he went back to the breakfast-table and sat down.

"Please don't sulk, Gordon," said Mother. "You've no idea how unpleasant your face looks when it sulks."

Gordon still looked sulky—but when he saw

Daddy's eye on him, over the top of the newspaper, he decided that he had better be sensible.

He remembered to brush his hair at dinner-time, and at tea-time, too. But when supper-time came he quite forgot! He arrived at the supper-table looking like a golliwog. Mother cried out when she saw him.

"Gordon! What *have* you been doing to your hair! It looks like a hedgehog's back!"

"Well, I've brushed it," said Gordon, telling a naughty story. "It must have got like that coming downstairs!"

That made Daddy cross. "You know what I said to you this morning, don't you?" he said sternly. "I said if you forgot again, you'd have to go without your Saturday five pence. Well, I shall keep my word. You

will have no five pence tomorrow morning—and the punishment is as much for telling a silly story as for disobeying Mother!"

Gordon was upset. He hadn't thought that Daddy had really meant what he said. The tears came into his eyes and he looked at Daddy to see if he would change his mind.

"It's no good looking at me like that," said Daddy. "I just think you're a cry-baby, that's all. I'm not pleased with you."

After supper Gordon went out into the garden to put away his bicycle. It was still daylight. Gordon put his bicycle into the shed and shut the door with a bang. He was in a temper.

"I meant to buy some sweets tomorrow—and I wanted my new *SUNNY STORIES*, too," he said, out loud. "Oh, bother my hair! I hate my hair! I wish I hadn't got hair like mine! Silly, stupid hair!"

"Well, let me do something about it for you," said a voice from somewhere nearby. Gordon looked about in surprise. He suddenly saw an ugly little fellow looking at him from under a laurel bush. Gordon thought it must be an imp or a goblin.

"Well, what can you do about it?" said the boy. "If you can do something which will stop me having to brush my hair half a dozen times a day, I'd be very glad. I'll give you my old bicycle bell, if you will. It still rings."

"Right!" said the goblin, eagerly. "Where is it?"

Gordon found it and gave it to the ugly little fellow. He stared up at Gordon out of bright green eyes. "I'm

going to say a spell," he said. "Stand still a minute, please. When the spell is over, you will never have the bother of brushing your hair again."

"Good!" said Gordon, and he stood perfectly still. His heart beat rather fast, for it was really very exciting to have such a thing happen to him.

"Imminy, pimminy, high in the air,
Off and away with your tiresome hair!"

chanted the little fellow. And Gordon felt a prickling and a tickling of his head—and to his enormous surprise he saw hundreds of dark brown hairs flying into the air and away!

He put his hand up to his head. It was bald and bare! He stared in dismay at the goblin.

"Now you'll never have to bother about brushing

your hair again!" said the goblin with a smile. "Isn't that good! Aren't you pleased?"

Gordon didn't answer. He rushed indoors and went to look at himself in the glass in the hall. How dreadful he looked! He hadn't a hair on his head. It was pink and bare—and felt very cold indeed!

"Oh dear! How terrible I look!" said poor Gordon. "What will Mother say! Whatever will all the boys at school say? I shall be laughed at all day long. I can't bear it. Oh, why did I grumble about brushing my hair? It's far more dreadful to have no hair to brush!"

The paper-boy came to the door and threw the paper on to the mat. The hall-door was open and the boy saw Gordon. He stared at him in surprise—and then he threw back his head and laughed loudly.

"Hallo, Baldy!" he said. "What have you done with your hair?"

Gordon ran into the garden again. He was frightened and upset. How silly that goblin was! Gordon hadn't meant him to take away his hair. He had only wanted hair that would look neat without being brushed.

"I wonder where the goblin is," thought the boy. "If I could find him, I'd make him give me back my hair—or get me some new hair, anyway."

He heard a ringing of a bell, and he knew it was the sound that his old bicycle bell made. He looked under the laurel bush and there he saw the goblin again—but this time he had a little friend with him, exactly like himself! He was showing him the bell, and the two of them were taking turns ringing it.

"Hie, goblin!" cried Gordon. "I want my hair back! I can't bear to have my head like this. Please give me back my hair!"

The goblin peeped out from the bush with bright sharp eyes. "How you do change your mind!" he said. "First you hate your hair—and then almost at once, you want it back again. Well—my friend here knows a spell to get it back—but he won't do it unless you give him a nice little bell like mine."

Gordon stared down in dismay. Both the little fellows looked up at him with sharp green eyes. They meant to drive a bargain with Gordon.

"All right," said the boy at last. "I'll give you my *new* bicycle bell—though I don't want to—*after* you've got back my hair, not before."

"Well, stand still whilst I say the spell," said the

second goblin. "I hope it will be your hair that comes back. It might be somebody else's, you know."

Gordon stood still. The goblin began to chant:

"Imminy, pimminy's what I said,
Hair, come back to the poor bald head!"

And, sure enough, through the air, thousands of little hairs came flying. They came back to Gordon's head and settled there. They grew once more—and there was the boy with a good thatch of hair again, feeling very pleased.

"I'll get you the bicycle bell," said Gordon, and rather sadly he unscrewed the nice bright new bell from his bicycle handle and gave it to the eager, green-eyed goblin. What a ringing there was under the laurel bush then! Both bells rang madly as the two goblins tried them over and over again.

Gordon went indoors and looked at himself in the glass. Yes—he looked better now—but what was this?

He looked closely at himself in the glass—and do you know what he saw? He had got all his own hair back again—and a tiny bit of somebody else's too! But instead of being dark brown, the somebody else's was golden! So just at the right side of Gordon's head was a little golden patch in his dark hair. Wasn't it queer?

"Oh, well, never mind, I expect it will grow dark," thought the boy. "My goodness me—I'll never forget to brush my hair again. I'm so glad to have it back. And to think I've lost both my bicycle bells, and my Saturday five pence, too, through being so silly about my hair!"

Mother was surprised at two things next day. She couldn't imagine how it was that Gordon had got a funny little golden bit in his hair—and she couldn't think why the little boy brushed his hair so well all of a sudden.

"I suppose it was because Daddy punished you," she said. "Well—if it makes you remember, it will be worth it. But I do wish I knew how that funny golden bit came there, Gordon."

Gordon didn't tell her because he was rather ashamed of himself. I wonder if you'll ever meet him. You'll know him if you do, because that golden bit never grew dark again! It's still there in his brown hair, like a small patch of magic sunlight!

The Disappearing Presents

"THE ONLY thing I don't like about Christmas time is having to write thank-you letters," said Peter. "They are an awful bore."

"Yes, they are," said Julie. "Still, if you sit down and make up your mind really to get on with them, they are soon done. You're lazy, Peter!"

"I wish I hadn't got to write any thank-you letters!" groaned Peter. "Such a waste of time! Mother, why do we have to?"

"For two reasons," said his mother, who saw sitting nearby with her sewing. "One is because it is only good manners to say thank you to someone kind enough to spend money on you and send a parcel—and the other reason is that of course the person who sends the present wants to know that you have got it safely."

"Bother good manners!" said Peter.

"Peter!" said his mother, sharply, "do you like people with bad manners? Do you like that boy who always pushes past you when you try to get on to the bus? Do you like that girl who calls rude names after you? Do you like Anna, who never says thank you

when she comes to tea, and never says please when she asks you to pass her the bread-and-butter?"

"No. I don't like any of them," said Peter, thinking.

"Nobody ever does like people with bad manners," said his mother. "Bad manners are simply selfishness —not caring in the least about other people or what they think of us. And writing thank-you letters is a form of good manners. You wouldn't dream of going out to tea, and then, when you say good-bye, forgetting to say thank you, would you?"

"Of course not," said Peter.

"Well, then, there's no difference between that and writing a thank-you letter," said his mother. "If the people you have to write letters to lived near enough for you to go and see them, and *say* thank you, you could do that—but they don't, so you must write. Now, I hope you understand."

"I'm only too glad to write and say thank you to Auntie Sue for sending me that dear little sewing-machine," said Julie, sitting down and getting out her notepaper. "I really do feel grateful to her for that. I can make all my dolls' clothes easily now."

"Well—I'll write my letters too," said Peter, feeling that his mother was quite right. It *was* ill-mannered and selfish not to write and say thank you. "Let me see—I must write to Uncle Fred for that engine—and Uncle John for the book—and Auntie Sue for the jigsaw—and Grandpa for the whistle—and Mrs. Parks for the book-token. Right. That's five. I'll do Grandpa first."

But before he had written more than "Dear Grandpa" a steam-roller went by outside and Peter ran to the window to see it. It stopped just outside, and one of the men got down to see to it. It took him about twenty minutes to put it right, and Peter watched all the time. Then, when he went back to his writing, it was dinner-time.

"Oh, well—I'll write the letters afterwards," thought Peter. But after dinner he picked up a book, and it was so exciting that he forgot all about his letters.

Julie had written all hers by the evening. She really stuck at it, and Mother was pleased with her. She read them all, and said yes, Julie could send them the next day. She had done them nicely.

"Well, Auntie Sue and the others deserved to have

nice thank-you letters," said Julie, "because they sent me such very nice things, Mother. How have you got on, Peter?"

"Oh—I didn't have time to do them to-day," said Peter, looking quickly at his mother. "I'll do them to-morrow."

He didn't do them the next day. Like all things that are put off, they were quite forgotten. Peter thought of them the day after—but he was just going out to play football with his friends, and he really couldn't be bothered to do them then. He would do them when he came in.

But he was tired when he came in, and the thought of writing five thank-you letters made him feel more tired still! So he didn't do them that day either.

On the fifth day Mother asked him a question. "Peter—how many thank-you letters have you done? Grandpa telephoned to-day to ask if you had got the beautiful whistle he sent you."

"Er—well, I haven't done many thank-you letters, I'm afraid," said Peter. "I really meant to do them to-day, Mother."

"I asked you how many you had done," said Mother, sternly.

"None," said Peter, going red. "I'll simply *have* to do them to-day."

"Come and show me them when you have written them," said Mother, and walked away, looking disgusted with Peter.

Well, you would have thought after that that Peter would certainly have sat down at the first chance he

had and written every single letter, wouldn't you? But he didn't. He put it off again, and not one got written that day.

The next day Peter had two friends to tea. They were Morris and William. "I'll show you my Christmas presents," said Peter. "My Grandpa sent me a marvellous whistle. Now where is it?

He couldn't find it though he hunted everywhere. How annoying. "Well, never mind," said Peter. "I'll show you my railway engine. Uncle Fred gave it to me. It's the finest one you ever saw."

But he couldn't find that either. How extraordinary! Julie had no idea where it was, either.

"Well—where's that jigsaw Auntie Sue gave me?" said Peter. "I saw that here yesterday morning. I haven't done it yet. We could all of us do it together."

But that had disappeared too! Peter simply couldn't understand it! Then he looked for the book that Uncle John had given him, and the book-token that his old nurse, Mrs. Parks, had sent him. But they were gone too. Peter was quite in despair.

He went to his mother. "Mother! I simply can't find five of my Christmas presents—my engine, my book, my book-token, my jigsaw puzzle and my whistle. Do you know where they are?"

"Oh, yes," said Mother. "I've sent them all back. I was so dreadfully ashamed of you for not having the good manners even to bother to sit down and spend five minutes on a thank-you letter, that I felt I must send back the presents. You don't deserve to keep them if you can't say thank you."

"Oh, Mother! But they were my presents!" said Peter, almost in tears. "That beautiful whistle!"

"Well—if you like to write to everyone and say how sorry you are for forgetting to write and say thank you, and tell them how much you liked the presents, and please would they be good enough to bring them next time they come and see you, maybe you could have them all again," said Mother. "That is the only thing I can suggest. I said how sorry I was that I hadn't a good-mannered boy—only a good-mannered girl."

Peter went back to Morris and William.

"What's up?" they said, seeing his gloomy face. Peter told them. William laughed.

"It's bad luck," he said. "But you deserve it. Golly, I wrote all my thank-you letters the very day after

Christmas. When did you write yours, Morris?"

"They took me two days," said Morris. "I had ten to write, you see. What are you going to do, Peter? Write and apologise and say you'd like them back?"

"I suppose so," said Peter, gloomily. "Take me far longer than saying thank you! Blow these thank-you letters."

"Well—you only let your mother down if you don't to the decent thing," said William. "You know what people say when children don't have manners—they say, 'Poor little thing, his mother's brought him up so badly he doesn't even know his manners! Mrs. So-and-So ought to learn a few manners herself, then her children would know how to behave'."

"Well! I wouldn't like that said about *my* mother!" said Peter, in horror. "My mother's got beautiful manners, she's awfully kind and unselfish and everyone likes her. You don't mean to say people might say beastly things about her if I don't behave well?"

"People *do*," said Morris. "I think your mother's sensible to send back your presents. At least everyone will know then that she did try to make you write your thank-you letters!"

Poor Peter! He wrote five most apologetic letters, which took him a very long time. I expect he *will* get all his presents back some time, but he does feel ashamed of himself. I hope your presents never disappear like that—but I'm sure you always write your thank-you letters quickly, like Julie does.